Booze and sexy conversation—that would be Tabitha's seduction technique.

She took a deep breath and widened her smile. "Did I ever tell you how interested the scribes were in the mating habits of various animals?"

Dev blinked. "No, I don't believe you did. A subject of great interest?"

Tabitha cleared her throat. She had started this and she was not going to falter now. "They thought partridges did it a bit too often. So much so that they often wore themselves out, poor birds."

"Fascinating."

"Lions were strongly approved of because they were thought to be loyal to their mate," Tabitha went on chattily. "There's not much information on the mating habits of dragons, though."

"Perhaps it's just as well."

"You're probably right," Tabitha agreed thoughtfully. "Some things are better left to the imagination."

STEPHANIE JAMES

is a pseudonym for bestselling, award-winning author **Jayne Ann Krentz**. Under various pseudonyms—including Jayne Castle and Amanda Quick—Ms. Krentz has over twenty-two million copies of her books in print. Her fans admire her versatility as she switches between historical, contemporary and futuristic romances. She attributes a "lifelong addiction to romantic daydreaming" as the chief influence on her writing. With her husband, Frank, she currently resides in the Pacific Northwest.

JAYNE ANN KRENTZ

WRITING AS
STEPHANIE JAMES

FABULOUS BEAST

Silhouette Books

Published by Silhouette Books
America's Publisher of Contemporary Romance

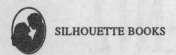 SILHOUETTE BOOKS

ISBN 0-373-80693-0

FABULOUS BEAST

For Suzanne, Barb and Elaine.
Friends in this business are not a luxury, but a
necessity. We are all committed to the same goal:
keeping each other sane.

One

"If you're the U.S. cavalry, you're a little late." The badly battered man with the silver eyes and the ebony cane managed a rather grisly parody of a smile before sliding slowly down the brick wall of the alley. He sank to his knees on the dirty cobblestones, bracing his shoulder against the bricks behind him. "But better late than never, I suppose."

The silver gaze was abruptly hidden by dark lashes as the man closed his eyes in pain. Although the extent of his injuries was obvious, he never relaxed the savage grip he had on the handle of the ebony cane.

Tabitha Graham, who had rounded the corner of the old alley only seconds before, stood staring in horrified shock at the sight of the beaten and bloody man. Her eyes widened in astounded recognition, and then she dropped the huge armload of packages she had been carrying.

"Oh, my God!" she breathed, heedless of the small fortune in souvenirs and trinkets she was abandoning in chaos at the entrance to the alley. She rushed forward, crouching at once beside the dark-haired man. "What happened?" Desperately she tried to remember her first aid.

There was a fair amount of blood on the man's khaki shirt and slacks as well as on his face, but he didn't seem to be bleeding profusely from any one deep wound. Tabitha held her breath, struggling to control her own shock and anxiety so that she could deal with the physical shock and pain the man must have been experiencing. No severe bleeding. And he was breathing, albeit painfully.

Taking a resolute grip on herself, Tabitha mentally ran through the list of vital signs to be checked first. It had been so long since she'd taken that first-aid class! Her hands moved on his kneeling figure, brushing gently over the broad shoulders and down to his waist, seeking the extent of the damage. When she lightly touched his rib cage, he gasped.

"Would you believe I walked into a brick wall?" he managed in an attempt at macabre humor. He didn't open his eyes. It seemed to be taking all his strength just to remain on his knees, leaning against the side of the alley.

"I might believe several people pushed you into that brick wall," Tabitha muttered as she finished the superficial inspection. "Here, lie down. You're not losing a great deal of blood and except for possibly a cracked rib, I don't think anything's broken. Are you feeling faint?"

"Hell, no. Women faint. Men pass out." He slumped a little farther down against the wall.

"Well, do you feel as if you're going to pass out?" Tabitha demanded, reaching out to steady him.

"Yes."

"Please. Lie down." She tried to ease him onto his side. "I think we should get your feet elevated. Don't want you going into shock. As soon as you're more comfortable I'll go for help."

"No!" The silver eyes flew open and she read the sudden command in them. "The ship sails in about half an hour, doesn't it?"

"Yes, but I don't think..."

"Listen. I'd rather be treated by the doctor on board the ship than risk getting stranded on this backwater island. Lord knows what kind of medical care is available here," he said urgently.

Tabitha chewed on her lip. "I'm not sure you should be moved."

"I'm damn well not going to spend the night in this alley!" He closed his eyes again and groaned as he changed position slightly. "Please. You're from the ship, too, aren't you?"

"Yes."

"I thought I'd seen you on board," he muttered. "Look, if you'll just help me get back to the wharf, I'd really appreciate it."

Tabitha frowned, realizing how important the matter was to him. He really didn't want to find himself stranded on the small Caribbean island where the cruise ship had docked for the afternoon. She couldn't blame him, she decided. If their positions had been reversed, she knew she'd rather trust herself to the medical care available on board the huge passenger ship than to the unknown facilities available locally.

"All right," she said reassuringly. "I'll find a way to get you back. Just stay still while I go flag down one of those crazy taxis."

He didn't answer; he didn't appear capable of answering. With a last anxious look at his hunched figure, Tabitha leaped to her feet and raced back toward the mouth of the alley. She nearly tripped over the sack containing the woven basket and the carved wooden dragon that had been among her last purchases.

Out on the narrow street she hailed the first small car which came into view. There was no need to worry about whether or not it was a taxi. One of the first things she had discovered when she'd gotten off the ship earlier in the day was that when a cruise ship was in town, every available car somehow metamorphosed into a taxi. The driver of this one screeched to a halt in front of her and grinned broadly.

"Taxi, lady?"

"Yes, but I need some help. There's another passenger. He's in the alley and he's been hurt. Will you give me a hand getting him into the car? We'll pay double the fare, naturally," she added quickly.

"Sure, lady." The man grinned even more cheerfully and jumped out of the somewhat banged-up automobile. "St. Regis very friendly island. Glad to help."

Without waiting, Tabitha turned and hurried back into the alley. The dark-haired man had sunk a little lower onto the cobblestones and his eyes were closed again. She could see the cold moisture on his brow and her sense of urgency increased. It was hot here on the island, but this man looked as if he were having chills. She noticed that his large hand was still clamped fiercely around the handle of the cane.

The cab driver whistled as he saw his other passenger. "Very bad. You need doctor, yes?"

"He wants the one on board the ship," Tabitha said hastily as the man with the cane tried to shake his head. It was obvious that the pain made the small movement sheer torture. "Here, give me a hand," she added and went forward to gently but firmly begin the difficult process of getting the battered man to his feet.

The car driver shrugged and obligingly stepped forward to help. Tabitha winced as she saw the whitening brackets on either side of the victim's hard mouth. The lines whitened even further as she and the taxi driver got him to his feet. But her fellow passenger said nothing as the three of them began the walk to the waiting car. Tabitha knew it was because it took his full willpower simply to make the journey.

Together she and the driver got the dark-haired man into the cab, and Tabitha slid into the back seat beside him. Her arm went around the man's shoulders in an instinctive effort to both comfort and steady him. She felt him stifle another groan of pain and then realized he was leaning heavily against her. His bruised face was turned into her shoulder and the brown lashes drooped against the high line of his cheek.

"Good medicine," the cab driver announced, reaching under his seat and withdrawing a small bottle of rum. He handed it back to Tabitha. "Give him some of this, lady. It help."

Doubtfully Tabitha took the bottle. "Do you really think he should have any alcohol?"

The silver eyes of the victim opened briefly, focusing on the rum bottle. "Definitely," he muttered huskily. He tried to raise a hand toward the bottle, but Tabitha moved it firmly out of reach and uncapped it. Then she painstakingly wiped the neck.

"All right, but just a small sip," she cautioned, holding the bottle to his lips. It was an unsteady process because of the manner in which the driver was whizzing the small car through the one main street of town toward the wharf. The vendors lining the street didn't even glance up from their wares as the car whipped past. They were accustomed to the local style of driving. The cruise ship would be leaving in less than half an hour and no one wanted to miss a last-minute sale. The street was rapidly emptying of tourists.

The dark-haired man swallowed the sip of rum Tabitha allowed and tried for another. Tabitha pulled the bottle back from his mouth. "I really don't think you should have any more," she explained anxiously.

He raised his silver eyes to meet her uncertain sherry brown gaze. "Please?" he whispered. "I hurt, lady. I hurt so much."

Knowing she could offer nothing else in the way of immediate relief, Tabitha relented. Her victim swallowed greedily from the bottle and then, without any warning, he collapsed completely. One moment he was drinking rum, the next he was sprawled across her lap, his dark head resting on her thigh.

"Oh, my God," Tabitha whispered. "Hurry, driver. *Hurry!*" She stared down at the man in her lap. The blood from the small cuts on his face was staining her white cotton pants. Her fingers fluttered soothingly along his wrist, seeking a pulse. The beat seemed reasonably strong, she discovered in relief. Her eyes wandered over his inert body once more.

She had seen the man more than once during the three days the cruise ship had been at sea, but always from a distance. She had no idea who he was. The ebony cane which he still grasped even in his semi-conscious state had always been in evidence when she had seen him on deck or in the dining room. It was a necessity, not an affectation, because the man walked with a decided limp.

He was heavy, lying across her legs, Tabitha thought fleetingly. Solid and hard and heavy but without an ounce of fat. Rather like a large, sleekly muscled animal. The dark, coffee brown hair was thick and cut conservatively in an apparent effort to tame a slight wave. The dark pelt was tousled now, a result of the violent activity the man had recently undergone, but the casual disarray of it did not make him look any younger. From a distance Tabitha had idly decided that he was probably almost forty and she saw nothing in him now to change that opinion.

In fact, Tabitha realized, up close the lines etched into his face indicated that he might even have passed his fortieth birthday. There was a fixed, implacable look about the aggressive nose and forceful jaw. The broadly carved features were neither sensitive nor aquiline. She could not read either intrinsic compassion or cruelty in the profile; simply a hard, unyielding strength. What had happened to his left leg to leave him with such a marked limp? she wondered. Perhaps an automobile accident.

What on earth had occurred in that miserable little alley? Had he been attacked by a group of young toughs who had been lying in wait for an unsuspecting tourist? With his limp and the evidence of the cane, this particular man might have seemed an especially easy target.

Curiously Tabitha reached into his pocket and found a worn leather wallet. Flipping it open, she discovered a Texas driver's license issued to one Devlin Colter. Whoever had assaulted him hadn't gotten the wallet, fortunately.

Devlin Colter. At least now he had a name. As the taxi came to a sliding halt in front of the docks, Tabitha hastily slid the wallet back into the pocket of Colter's khaki slacks. He stirred as she did so, reacting apparently to the cessation of motion rather than to the fact that she had been going through his pockets. Tabitha suddenly felt a little guilty.

"We're at the ship," she murmured soothingly. Her fingers gently stroked his arm. "I'll ask them to bring out a stretcher."

"Please don't," he muttered thickly. "This is going to be embarrassing enough as it is. Just help me out of the cab, will you?"

"Of course, but I really think…"

Devlin Colter didn't appear to be paying much attention to what she thought. His whole concentration was on getting to a sitting position. She heard him swear feelingly as he managed the feat. Then the cab driver was jumping out to assist his double-fare passengers.

Two of the cruise ship's crew lounging near the gangway saw Tabitha and her fellow passenger and hurried forward to assist.

"Have the doc paged, Emerson," one of the men said briskly as he took the weight of Devlin Colter. "And notify the captain. Looks like one of our passengers met up with an accident on shore." His eyes narrowed as he turned to glance at Tabitha. "Car accident?"

"No, at least I don't think so. I found him like this in an alley near the main market area. I think he's been beaten up by some punks."

"Yeah, that's what it looks like. We've never had any trouble on St. Regis before," the crewman said unhappily as he and another man guided the stumbling Colter toward the gangway. "Here, you take his cane. It's in the way."

"No," Colter growled through clenched teeth as he fought for consciousness. "I'll keep it."

Tabitha's heart twisted as she witnessed his desperate need to hang on to the ebony stick. In a moment of crisis some people cling irrationally to seemingly insignificant objects. The cane had probably come to be an extension of himself over the years, and Colter undoubtedly felt awkward and unsteady without it.

"I'll take good care of it," she promised gently, taking hold of the cane. "And right now it really is in the way." For an instant she didn't think he was going to surrender it. As he stood braced by the two members of the ship's crew, Devlin Colter opened his silver eyes wide enough to regard Tabitha through two narrow slits. He seemed to realize he was in no shape to fight this small battle.

"Take it," he muttered. "But stay with me. Give me your word that you'll stay with me for a while."

Tabitha was oddly touched at the stark pleading in his low, rough voice. She answered without thinking. "I'll stay with you as long as you want me."

The silver eyes pinned her for a timeless, assessing moment. And then, apparently satisfied at what he had seen, Colter gritted, "Yes, you will, won't you?" As if the decision to trust her with his cane sapped the remainder of what little energy he had left, Colter slipped into a faint.

No, Tabitha reminded herself as she followed the two crewmen who were carrying him, Colter hadn't fainted, he'd passed out. She clung very tightly to the ebony cane.

Two hours later she was still obediently clutching the cane as she sat beside the white-sheeted bed in the small but well-equipped sick bay. Devlin Colter had wandered in and out of consciousness while the ship's doctor tended to his wounds, but each time he had stirred restlessly and opened his silvery eyes, he'd caught sight of Tabitha nearby and the image had appeared to reassure him. Now he was sleeping, a reasonably normal sort of sleep thanks to a sedative. His body bore several strips of tape and bandages and there were dark bruises under his eyes. The ribs, fortunately, had only been battered, not broken, although the doctor said they would cause considerable discomfort for several days. Still, all things considered,

Devlin Colter was in fair shape for a man who had undergone a severe beating in a back alley.

What was it about the sight of her which had calmed him during his restless moments? Tabitha wondered fleetingly as she sat holding the cane. He had seemed lucid when he was awake so she didn't think he was hallucinating. He didn't seem to be mistaking her for someone else.

Not that she was the kind of person who generally got mistaken for someone else, Tabitha reminded herself dryly. If anything, people were more inclined to overlook her altogether. Quiet people often got overlooked. Sometimes that suited them perfectly. Sometimes it was frustrating.

A quiet woman who was hauntingly beautiful probably wouldn't have known what it was like to spend most of her life as an observer of others. She would probably have been considered tragic and vulnerable and in need of a man's protection. Some male would have long since swept her off her feet.

But Tabitha Graham had not reached the age of twenty-nine years without learning that she was not the hauntingly beautiful, tragically quiet type. Instead she felt rather average when it came to looks. Her toast-colored hair was cropped in a blunt cut which swung gently along the line of her jaw, neither short and sassy nor long and sultry in style.

The light brown hair framed a set of features that were softly molded, almost wholesome. Wholesome was a word Tabitha didn't care for at all, even if it did suit her gentle mouth and slightly tilted nose.

It was the sherry-colored eyes which somewhat mitigated the wholesome effect. They were faintly slanted at the outer corners, and there was a flare of intelligence and humor in them which could not be completely dimmed.

As far as the rest of her was concerned, Tabitha had to admit that the term wholesome probably was as accurate as any. Unfortunately. There was a soft roundness to her breasts and hips which no amount of dieting ever seemed to diminish. All dieting managed to achieve, Tabitha had long since realized, was a stalemate in the battle against outright plumpness. The endless food available on board a luxury cruise liner was not contributing to the war effort. Or if it was, it was definitely on the wrong side. But that was all right, she had assured herself three days ago. This was supposed to be a vacation and she was entitled to enjoy it.

With that thought in mind, she had purchased loose-fitting cottons for the Caribbean cruise, clothing that would not remind her of how much she was enjoying the food. Her white, drawstring pants which were now stained with blood and dirt were accompanied by a square-necked, handkerchief-hem, white top. The only jewelry Tabitha had on was a silver pendant designed in the shape of a griffin. The small sculpture with its lion's body and eagle's head was a fierce little creature drawn from the pages of a medieval bestiary. As she absently fingered the beast, Tabitha abruptly remembered the tiny, dragon carving she had left lying at the entrance to the old alley.

It wasn't the only souvenir she had left on the cobblestones in her haste to rescue Devlin Colter, but it was the one she would miss the most. It had been an especially charming beast with a handsome head and delicately detailed claws. Ah, well, Colter was an even more interesting beast, she thought humorously. A small, private smile curved her mouth just as his silver eyes flickered open.

"Don't worry, I've still got it," she assured him, holding up the cane.

His gaze went briefly from her face to the cane and back again. "Thanks," he said seriously. "Thanks for everything. I owe you."

Tabitha shook her head, smiling. "Don't be ridiculous. Anyone would have done the same. I just happened to be the first tourist passing that alley after you got clobbered in it. Which reminds me. The captain would like to talk to you when you're feeling up to a chat. I guess he's got a few questions about what happened. The steamship company doesn't like having its passengers beaten up while visiting places like St. Regis. Whoever it was didn't get your wallet, by the way."

Devlin continued to stare at her for another moment. The weakness and sedative-induced drowsiness in him was obvious. "I suppose I should be grateful for small favors," he managed dryly. "Who are you, anyway?"

"Tabitha Graham. From Washington."

"D.C.?"

She grimaced. "State of. Every traveling citizen of the state of Washington has to explain that for some reason! People always assume the D.C."

He nodded once and then winced as the motion apparently sent a wave of discomfort through his head. "You look more like the state of than D.C."

The silver eyes closed for a moment as he took a couple of careful breaths.

"How can you tell?" Tabitha asked curiously.

He didn't open his eyes. "I used to live there. D.C. types are a little harder, a little more…" His voice trailed off as he searched for a word.

"Sophisticated?" Tabitha supplied dryly.

"I guess. You look sort of soft." His eyes were still closed.

"Wholesome? Healthy? Sweet?" she added help-fully.

"Yeah. Maybe." He was clearly tiring; losing interest in the analysis. That didn't surprise Tabitha. She was accustomed to men losing interest. Just as she thought he was drifting back into sleep, however, the silver gray eyes slitted open once more. "What do you do up in the state of Washington, Tabitha Graham?"

"I run a small bookshop in a little town on Puget Sound. It's a wholesome, healthy, sweet sort of occupation," she confided cheerfully. "What about you?"

There was a small pause. She didn't know whether he was simply assimilating her words or whether he had actually fallen asleep. Then Colter said quietly, "I have an equally wholesome, sweet and, until now, healthy occupation. I run a travel agency."

"Uh oh. Let me guess. You're going to take St. Regis off your list of recommended tourist stops as soon as you get home, right?"

"The temptation is strong."

"What happened in that horrible little alley, Devlin?" she inquired softly.

"Call me Dev." He paused again, gathering his strength. "I'm afraid it was exactly what it looks like. I got clobbered by a couple of young toughs who were anxious to supplement their annual income."

"Well, they didn't get your money!" Tabitha exclaimed in satisfaction.

"That is, of course, a great comfort," he muttered. "Frankly, I'd rather they had asked politely for the traveler's checks I was carrying instead of trying to take them off me the hard way. You'd better tell the captain I'm awake."

Tabitha got to her feet and stepped closer to the bed, frowning down at him intently. "Are you sure you're ready to talk to him?"

"I'm sure." He slanted a glance up at her serious expression. "Hang on to my cane for me, will you? I don't seem to be in any condition to hang on to it myself."

She smiled reassuringly. "I'll keep track of it for you. Do you want anything else before I leave?"

"A small bottle of whiskey would be much appreciated."

"Oh no, I don't think so. Not on top of all those pain-killers you've got in you," Tabitha said quickly.

"The pain-killers leave something to be desired. Please?" He tried a tentative, ingratiating smile that amused Tabitha.

"No. I'm sure the doctor would never approve. Now you get some rest while I go tell the nurse you're awake. She can notify the captain." Tabitha smiled again and touched his arm as it lay under the sheet. Then she turned quickly and started for the door.

"Tabby!" he called after her, sounding suddenly concerned.

"Tabby?" she echoed, swinging around in surprise as she reached the door. Her brows came together in a straight line.

"Sorry," Dev apologized at once. "Something about you reminds me of a tabby cat." He lifted one hand in a vague gesture of explanation.

"Uh huh. Sweet and wholesome. What did you want, Dev?"

"I just wanted to remind you of the cane."

She shook her head. "Believe me, I won't let it out of my sight." Grasping it firmly, she continued out the door. He really was fixated on the ebony cane, she thought with a touch of compassion. The poor man must feel terribly uncertain and unsteady without it. His limp made him vulnerable, she realized as she went about the business of notifying the nurse that the patient was awake. Tabitha didn't know many vulnerable men. It was intriguing to meet one.

She was still considering that notion an hour later in her cabin as she dressed for dinner. The easy-fitting, yellow pullover dress she had chosen was both comfortable and reasonably attractive. There was nothing startlingly chic about it, but on the other hand it wouldn't embarrass her, either. A perfect Tabitha sort of outfit, she decided as she brushed her hair into the familiar soft curve. It wouldn't draw attention.

She hesitated for a moment after setting down the brush and then decided to exchange the silver griffin pendant for a wide brass bracelet which had a small unicorn engraved on it. Then, satisfied, she picked up her purse and prepared to leave the tiny stateroom.

She had her hand on the doorknob when the phone on the night table rang shrilly. Tabitha blinked in surprise. She didn't know anyone else on board ship well enough to expect a call. Someone had probably dialed the wrong room. She lifted the receiver a little impatiently.

"Tabby?"

She arched an eyebrow in astonishment, identifying that low, rough voice at once. "It's okay, Dev," she half-chuckled. "I've still got your cane. It's safe and sound."

"Oh. Well, thanks, but that's not exactly what I was calling about. I was wondering if you might consider bringing me a little soup or something."

"Soup! Didn't the nurse order dinner for you?"

"I'm not in sick bay any longer. I'm back in my cabin. I couldn't stand any more of the antiseptic look."

"Are you sure you shouldn't have spent the night there?" Tabitha demanded. "After all, you've got a lot of recovering to do."

"I can do it just as well here in my cabin. If I can get a little food, that is," he added meaningfully. "What about it? Do you think you could wangle a little something from the kitchens?"

"I can try," she agreed slowly, wondering why he simply didn't call a steward. Maybe he just didn't feel up to explaining why he wanted to be served in his cabin tonight. He did sound awfully weak. "Okay, I'll see what I can do. What's your cabin number?"

He told her and then hung up the phone, sounding more exhausted than ever. Tabitha replaced her own receiver thoughtfully. The poor man was apparently traveling alone, just as she was. And just like herself, he didn't seem to have made any friends on board, at least none he felt he could call upon in a situation like this. Tabitha felt herself warming toward Devlin Colter. He appeared to be a quiet, self-contained person who was not accustomed to imposing on people. A person who did not fit easily into the cheerful social life on board the cruise ship.

A person rather like herself.

It took some explanations and a short discussion with a member of the purser's staff, but Tabitha eventually arranged for dinner to be served to Devlin and herself in his cabin. She felt a small sense of triumph as she knocked on his door half an hour later with a steward in tow.

His voice was groggy as he instructed her to enter, and she realized at once that he wasn't looking any better. Lying in bed, naked from the waist up except for assorted bandages, Dev appeared more bruised and battered than she had last seen him. Tabitha halted on the threshold of the room, eyeing him dubiously. His precious cane was in her hand.

"Are you sure you shouldn't be in sick bay?" she asked.

"I'm sure," he growled, his eyes running over her almost curiously as she walked into the room. "The bruises are just starting to color up a little, that's all. They'll look even worse tomorrow." He watched her set down his cane.

"You sound like an expert on the subject," she noted dryly as she motioned for the steward to carry in the tray full of food she had selected.

Dev's gaze went from her to the tray as the steward

set it down on the small table by the bed. "Good grief, I ordered soup. You look like you've brought along a full-course dinner."

"The clam chowder is for you. The rest of the food is for me." Tabitha smiled, remembering to tip the steward as he backed out of the door.

"You're eating here with me?" Dev glanced at her interestedly. "I appreciate that. It's a little lonely down here all by myself."

"I figured it might be. Let's see what we have. Can you sit up in bed?"

"With a little help."

"Oh, of course." She stepped across the short expanse of space and carefully placed her arm around his shoulders. The feel of his warm skin elicited an unexpected sense of awareness in her. She felt the movement of the sleek, hard muscles of his shoulders as he groaned and struggled awkwardly to a sitting position. His masculine strength coupled with the feel of his bronzed skin made her abruptly nervous. As he settled into the pillows, she moved back quickly, nearly bumping into the tray full of food.

"Careful, that was my chowder that almost fell on the rug," he observed casually.

"Sorry," she mumbled and quickly turned her attention to preparing his soup. By the time she had it placed on his lap together with a chunk of sourdough bread, Tabitha was feeling in command of herself once again. It was obvious her touch hadn't had the same unsettling effect on Dev as the feel of his body had had on her! The man was in absolutely miserable shape, she reminded herself forcefully. The last thing he would be thinking about right at the moment was his own semi-nudity. And even if he had been, she thought good-naturedly, it didn't follow that her touch would necessarily spark a chord of awareness in him. Men didn't react that way to her even when they were in prime condition!

"Oh good," Dev was saying with a genuine trace of enthusiasm in his voice. "You brought along some wine."

"That's for me, too." She chuckled, busying herself with the dishes on the tray. "It's to go with my lobster pâté and my fettuccini." She uncovered the last of her own dishes, a spinach salad, and glanced up in time to catch an appalled expression on Dev's face.

"You're going to sit there, eat all that good food and drink all that excellent wine in front of me without even offering a bite or a sip?"

"You said you only wanted soup," she pointed out calmly, arranging her chair at the little table.

"I think I've changed my mind," he countered weakly, his eyes following her hands as she carefully poured out a glass of wine.

"I thought you might," Tabitha agreed with a satisfied nod. "That's why I ordered double on the fettuccini and had the steward bring along another wineglass." She produced the second glass from behind a silver tureen and smiled appealingly. "I checked with the doctor, and he said the drugs should have worn off sufficiently by now to allow you some alcohol."

He sighed in exaggerated relief. "For a minute there I was beginning to suspect there might be a cruel streak beneath that wholesome, sweet facade!"

Tabitha laughed lightly as she handed him a toast

point covered with pâté. "I enjoy good food too much to deny it to someone else. Given your present condition, though, there's not much you could have done about it if I'd chosen to sit here and torment you by eating every last scrap myself."

He winced. "You've got a point there. I couldn't wrest that wine bottle away from a fly tonight. Damn, but I ache! All over, too. Even my feet seem to hurt. Look at this," he added in outright disgust as he picked up his soup spoon, "my hand is shaking. Of all the stupid, idiotic..."

"It's just reaction to the shock your body's been through," Tabitha said soothingly, and rose instantly to cross back to his side. "Here, I'll help you." She took the spoon from his unsteady grasp and began ladling up the chowder and holding it to his lips.

"When I ordered dinner, I didn't expect to have it hand-fed to me," Dev groaned. But he downed the soup with definite enthusiasm. By the time they got to the fettuccini he was feeling strong enough to handle his own fork.

Tabitha watched the process with a sense of pleased satisfaction. If she hadn't taken it upon herself to order the remainder of the meal, her patient would only have had some soup tonight. Not nearly enough for a man his size. Half-amused at the gentle, nurturing impulse she was feeling toward Devlin Colter, she magnanimously gave him the last of the beaujolais wine.

"Wow, that tasted good." He sighed, leaning back farther into the pillows as she took the empty glass from his hand. "I was a lot hungrier than I thought.

And that wine is a lot more help than the doctor's pain pills!''

"You look exhausted," she informed him, arranging the empty dishes on the tray. "What you need now is some sleep."

"Yes, I know. But it's rather nice to have someone to talk to tonight. Any chance of your staying for a while?"

She turned in surprise to find him watching her with a shuttered, half-pleading expression. He really did want her to stay. Perhaps the shock of being so badly beaten by a band of thugs left even a strong man like this feeling uneasy at the thought of facing a long night of pain alone. "I'll stay for a while if you like," she murmured gently. "Would you like to play cards or something?"

"No." He shook his head a little restlessly. "Just...talk to me, okay? I'm sure I'll fall asleep fairly quickly."

She got the unspoken message. He wanted her to stay until he was asleep. Moving her chair closer to the bed, she instinctively put out a hand to touch his brow. "How's your head?"

"Hurts like hell, just like the rest of me," he admitted gruffly. He turned his face slightly toward her in a move that brought his forehead more firmly against her palm. "Your hand feels cool. Nice."

"Maybe a damp washcloth would help." Tabitha pulled her hand away, aware once more of that faint trace of unease she experienced whenever she touched him. Rising, she went into the small bath and located a washcloth. When she returned a few minutes later to place the dampened cloth on his forehead, his dark lashes were drooping, veiling the silver eyes. He was clearly exhausted.

When she draped the cloth across his brow he groaned a small sigh of relief. "Feels good," he mumbled without opening his eyes. He groped for a moment with his hand, found hers and placed her fingertips against his temple. "That's where it hurts the most."

Tabitha chewed uncertainly on her lower lip for an instant and then realized that all she really wanted to do was help relieve his pain. Carefully she began massaging his temple. He responded with another muttered sigh, and she sensed his body relaxing. The hard, set lines of his face eased a little and the dark lashes stayed closed. Such an unhandsome face, she thought wonderingly, but such beautiful eyes. Like a dragon.

The image that thought produced caused her lips to curve upward in another of her private, little smiles. It was some time before she realized Dev had fallen asleep.

For a few moments longer she continued to massage his temple, and then she carefully withdrew her hand. It was time to go back to her own cabin.

"No." It was a husky plea, thick with sleep. Her hand was caught in his and pushed back to his head. Then Dev shifted slightly, the restlessness evidence of the pain which still assaulted his body.

She couldn't leave him yet. He needed her. Tabitha took a deep breath and moved from the chair to sit beside him on the bed. It would be easier to go on massaging his head from that position.

As if he sensed that she wasn't going to abandon

him to a lonely night of discomfort, Dev Colter fell
more soundly asleep. Tabitha stared down at him,
aware that she had a strange, protective feeling toward
this man who was still very much a stranger. Perhaps
because she had been the one to rescue him from that
dirty alley and get him safely back to the ship; perhaps because he seemed to need her care tonight.
Whatever the reason, she felt a strong desire to soothe
and comfort him. He needed her. No man had ever
really needed her before.

His vulnerability was new to her. She found it appealing in an unexpected fashion. It made him seem
unthreatening and hinted at a sensitivity which most
men seemed to lack.

Tabitha realized that she could like Devlin Colter
very much, and the knowledge sent a wave of plea-
surable warmth through her. She would take good
care of him.

Two

*T*abby cat.

She lay curled beside him on the narrow bed looking for all the world like a soft, purring tabby cat.
Except that she wasn't exactly purring, Dev corrected
himself, as he examined the woman beside him. She
was sound asleep. What would it take to make her
purr?

He kept very still on his side of the bed, watching
as the Caribbean dawn began to filter through the
stateroom window. He realized wryly that he wasn't
avoiding movement just because of a reluctance to
reawaken the aches and pains of yesterday in his stiff
muscles, but rather because he was strangely reluctant
to awaken Miss Tabitha Graham. He knew that when
those huge sherry-colored eyes opened, they were going to be filled with acute embarrassment and with
that watchful, distant caution he had seen in them

yesterday and once or twice during the preceding three days.

Dev decided he rather liked her the way she was now, her soft, satisfyingly curved body curled in a relaxed and trusting sprawl alongside him. It took an effort of will to resist the temptation to reach out and stroke the full line of her sweet derriere. But he realized that if he gave in to the urge she would undoubtedly awaken, and he wanted to delay that event as long as possible.

It wasn't just the rounded curve of her rear which intrigued him; Miss Tabitha Graham also had a pleasantly full bosom. The old-fashioned word made him smile unexpectedly. He straightened his mouth almost at once when the expression tugged painfully at bruised and cut flesh. But his gaze continued to linger on the outline of Tabitha's breasts beneath the cotton knit dress. It would be interesting to see how the soft mounds reacted to a man's touch.

No, he decided with an unusual restlessness, not just to a man's touch; to *his* touch. Would the nipples harden into small, dark pebbles? If he succeeded in eliciting a reaction like that would she then part her soft, rounded thighs and let him slide between them?

Hell, what was the mater with him this morning? Here he was, stiff and sore in every muscle and his mind insisted on busying itself with a fantasy which, if actually carried out, would prove to be sheer torture to his bruised frame. Not to mention the fact that it would undoubtedly scare Miss Tabitha Graham right back to her own stateroom, never to re-emerge for the duration of the voyage.

And it occurred to Dev that that was the last thing

he wanted to do. He didn't want his tabby cat to disappear; she was proving to be very pleasant to have around. There was something infinitely comforting and soothing about her presence, and he was unfamiliar with comforting and soothing women.

When she had rounded the corner of that alley yesterday, he had sensed almost immediately that she wasn't going to panic or flutter about uselessly. After the initial shock of seeing his battered condition, she had dropped everything, literally, and come to his rescue. He had known as soon as he felt her gentle touch on his aching body that she could be trusted. How he knew that, he couldn't have said. Dev Colter had not made a lifelong habit of trusting people, but he had learned to trust his instincts. They had kept him alive this long.

On the way back to the ship he had let himself be comforted by the warmth and softness of her body. He could still remember the shape of her thigh beneath his cheek as he'd sprawled on her lap. When he'd awakened from the doctor's ministrations, it had been reassuring to see her sweetly anxious face light up with that gentle smile. No woman had ever looked at him quite like that before. The urge to call her with a plea for dinner later had been irresistible.

Dev's mouth hardened grimly as he realized what the direction of his thoughts was doing to his body. Perhaps it was normal for a man to have a few fantasies when he woke up to find a woman, any woman, lying beside him! And when that woman was the same creature who had rescued him and comforted him, perhaps it was even more normal to do a little fantasizing.

But regardless of the normalness of the situation, Dev had enough perception to know that throwing himself on top of Miss Tabitha Graham, even if he had been physically capable of the action this morning, would only result in unmitigated disaster. She'd flee and that was the last thing he wanted.

Dev Colter was discovering that he was hungry for more of the gentle, soothing comfort he had received yesterday. In fact, he wanted a hell of a lot more of it. It was not a commodity which had been particularly abundant in his life. At forty he was suddenly aware that he was rather greedy for what he had missed. He had enough self-control not to jeopardize his present good luck by giving in to the urgings of his body. When Tabitha stirred slightly, he instantly closed his eyes. He'd trust his instincts in dealing with her.

She awoke with a feeling of disorientation. For a moment Tabitha delayed opening her eyes, trying to assimilate the elements of strangeness which were impinging on her. The steady, throbbing feel of the ship's engines was familiar enough, but nothing else seemed quite right. For one thing there was a solid, warm body next to hers on the bed. Tabitha's eyes flew open in alarm as reality came back with a thud.

For an agonizing instant she lay perfectly still, hardly daring to seek out Dev Colter's face. What must he be thinking? How could she have fallen asleep like that last night? There was a distant recollection of easing herself down beside him so that she could rest a little while she massaged his temple and then nothing until now. How excruciatingly embarrassing for both of them!

But when she found the nerve to raise her eyes to his face, she heaved a sigh of relief. He was still asleep. Her incipient embarrassment faded to be replaced by concern. Poor man. He must be exhausted. Thank heaven he had been able to get some rest.

Carefully Tabitha eased herself out of the narrow bed, aware of a distinct feeling of purely feminine pleasure. What rest Dev had obtained was attributable, in part, to her. Hurriedly she collected her sandals, which had apparently fallen off during the night, and slipped out of the stateroom.

A hasty glance up and down the corridor determined that no one was witnessing her early morning departure from a man's room. Not that anyone on board would particularly care, she assured herself wryly as she made her way back to her own deck. Everyone on board was there to enjoy himself or herself to the fullest and certainly wouldn't begrudge others doing the same!

But Tabitha was not accustomed to making any kind of spectacle of herself and the thought of someone smirking over her departure from a man's cabin was enough to bring a wave of warmth to her cheeks. She hated scenes of any kind and she was especially horrified at the thought of finding herself the center of speculative attention. She liked to think it was because she was sensitive, but the simple truth was that she lacked the self-confidence to carry off such a situation and she knew it.

With a vast sense of relief she gained the privacy of her own stateroom. A nice, hot shower would restore her usual calm, she decided at once, stripping off the yellow cotton knit dress. Catching sight of her nude body just before she stepped into the bath, she gave a self-mocking smile. What would Dev Colter have thought if he'd awakened to find her lying next to him?

Would he have found anything at all appealing in her gently rounded frame? Probably not. Tabitha sighed philosophically. She had learned long ago that while men sometimes admired full breasts and hips, she apparently lacked the sensual voluptuousness which made such a shape truly attractive. And her ex-husband had made it abundantly clear that she also lacked the fiery, ardent nature which might have compensated.

Grimacing, she went into the shower and turned on the water. As soon as she was out she would order breakfast for Dev. He had been hungry last night and presumably would be again this morning. He needed to eat for strength, she decided determinedly, and immediately began planning a strengthening sort of menu for him. It was quite pleasant to lose herself in the activity, and it restored her equilibrium.

By the time she knocked on his door half an hour later she was feeling quite in command of herself and of the situation. His answering invitation to enter seemed to come with reassuring alacrity.

"Good morning," Tabitha said cheerfully as she walked into the room, once again followed by a steward carrying a tray. "How are you feeling? I've brought breakfast."

Dev was sitting on the edge of the bed, dressed in a fresh pair of light tan pants clasped around his hard waist with a dark leather belt. Contrasting with the bandages he still wore, his nude upper torso was sleek and bronzed in the early morning light, and his dark brown hair had been brushed into place. It still bore a trace of dampness from the shower. His silvery eyes focused on her immediately.

"Great. I'm starving again. I was just wondering whether or not I had enough strength left after that shower to make it up to the dining room. It was very thoughtful of you to do this, Tabby."

Tabitha glowed at the genuine note of gratitude in his voice. Such a nice man, she thought happily. Polite, grateful for small favors, sensitive, vulnerable. For what more could a woman ask? Perhaps this sort of man wouldn't care if a woman's roundness couldn't exactly be described as voluptuous?

"Do you need any more pain pills?" she asked, airily dismissing the steward so that she could dish up the grapefruit and scrambled eggs herself. "I can ask the doctor for another packet, if you like." She uncovered a plate of toast, peering down at it to make sure the cook had remembered to butter the bread.

"I think I'll survive on aspirin today," he murmured, watching as she bustled about the tray.

Aware of his eyes following her every move, Tabitha hastened through her preparations and then motioned him to the chair on the opposite side of the small table. What a relief to know he had still been asleep when she'd awakened this morning!

"I've been trying to decide whether or not you should spend the day in bed," she told him as he cautiously sat down across from her. "It's obvious you're still not feeling very well."

"I still ache a bit here and there," he admitted. "But I think the sun might feel good on my poor, battered body. What do you think?" he asked humbly.

"You might be right," she agreed thoughtfully. "The warmth might be good for those aching muscles. We'll fill you full of aspirins after breakfast and then go find a couple of vacant deck chairs near the pool. How does that sound?"

She thought she saw a flash of something close to relief in his eyes before he nodded and agreed. "It sounds delightful." He paused and then went on softly, "I haven't thanked you for helping me get to sleep last night, Tabby."

She blinked in sudden uncertainty. How much did he remember about last night? In the next moment she relaxed as he gave her a blandly polite look. "It was quite all right. You don't owe me any thanks. I was glad to do it. What did the captain say when you told him what had happened on St. Regis?"

Dev shrugged and then stifled a small groan, regretting the movement. "He said he'd check back with the local authorities but that probably not much would be done. This sort of thing happens occasionally everywhere in the world. I should never have wandered down that alley in the first place," he added ruefully.

"How were you to know it would be dangerous?" she countered roundly. "Heavens, I was about to do the exact same thing. A few minutes earlier and it would have been me who got attacked."

The level glance he gave her was suddenly unreadable. "How did you happen to wander into that alley when you did?" He dug into his grapefruit.

"I was following a sign on the wall outside which said there was a sculptor's studio at the other end," she explained easily. "I had already found the most interesting little wooden dragon at another shop, and I was hoping to find something else equally fascinating before I went back to the ship. You never can tell what will turn up at little, hidden shops."

"What sort of things do you collect?" he asked curiously.

"Things like this," she said, holding out her hand to display a ring done in an intricate design.

Dev frowned over her fingers. "What is it?"

"A sea serpent! Can't you see the little fins and the odd-shaped head?"

"Er, yes, now that you mention it. Uh, you collect sea serpents?" he asked very politely.

Tabitha smiled in amusement. "I like fantastic creatures. Dragons and unicorns and griffins and harpies. There's something about mythological animals that I find fascinating. I can't really explain it."

"Maybe it's because you're part tabby cat," he suggested softly.

She looked up in surprise and then chuckled. "Tabby cats are hardly fantastic creatures. Quite ordinary animals, as a matter of fact."

"Any creature is fantastic to someone who isn't familiar with it. If a man had never seen a tabby cat up close, he might be quite amazed when one wandered into his life." Dev's words were spoken in a slow, thoughtful tone.

Tabitha stared at him in astonishment. "You're absolutely right, you know,' she said very seriously, plunging into her favorite topic. "When the medieval monks wrote their bestiaries they had to describe a lot of creatures they had never seen. It was natural that the unfamiliar ones seemed quite strange to them."

"Bestiaries?" he queried.

"Books of beasts," she laughed. "They were books of natural history. Full of information on flora and fauna. They were serious attempts at biology but a lot of the information on animals from far-off lands got a little garbled in the translation process. Perfectly understandable, of course, given the limited methods of communication at the time. It's rather fun to sit down with a bestiary and figure out just what kind of creature a griffin or a unicorn really is."

"What do the bestiaries have to say about tabby cats?" Dev's mouth crooked into a small smile, and his eyes asked her to share the humor.

"Not much, as I recall," she retorted dryly. "Something about cats being useful for catching mice, I think. It's a very short entry in most bestiaries. Perhaps a case of familiarity breeding contempt." Determinedly Tabitha decided to take charge of the conversation. She didn't care for the personal tone it seemed to be assuming. "Are you on board this ship to scout out new itineraries for your clients?"

He hesitated as if reluctant to change the topic and then gave in gracefully. "That's right. One of the perks of being in the travel business."

"Have you been in the field long?"

"Quite a while," he answered vaguely.

"You must have seen a great deal of the world by now," she said enthusiastically.

"A fair amount," he agreed dryly. "Is this your first cruise?"

"How can you tell?" she asked, grinning.

"You seem to be a little reluctant to join in with the others. I've noticed you a few times during the past couple of days, and you're always by yourself."

She flushed. "I could say the same thing about you."

He looked pleased. "Had you noticed me before you encountered me in that alley yesterday then?"

Something about the boyish pleasure in his eyes made her laugh out loud. "Yes, as a matter of fact, I had."

"It's the cane," he decided, abruptly morose. "People tend to notice a man with a limp."

"If you think they noticed you when you had a limp, just wait until they get a load of you covered in bandages and bruises!" she teased gently.

He muttered something in disgust. "You've just convinced me to spend the day in the cabin instead of on deck."

"Nonsense," she scolded roundly. "I think you're quite right. The sun will feel good, and I refuse to let you sulk down here in your cabin when going topside is bound to be therapeutic. Besides, with a shirt on, the only visible marks are going to be the bruises on your cheek and under your eye. They'll give you a mysterious, dangerous look. Very appealing to the ladies. Just wait and see."

"I'm on board for business purposes," he stated aloofly, "not to appeal to the ladies.'

Sensing that she had somehow offended him, Tabitha impulsively reached across the table to touch his hand. "I'm sorry. I was only teasing you." When he nodded a bit shortly, accepting her apology, she quickly withdrew her hand. His eyes went to where her fingers had rested on his skin, and then he picked up his fork and resumed eating the scrambled eggs.

Tabitha smiled happily to herself. She really did like this man who was capable of being embarrassed at the thought of serving as a titillating source of interest to women. Such a pleasure to encounter a male whose ego wasn't overly inflated! And she could empathize with him completely. She would have reacted exactly the same way if someone had intimated she might be capable of drawing the attention of the males on board.

The day ahead stretched forth invitingly. With a strong sense of proprietary interest in the man she had rescued, Tabitha took charge of the day's activities. Dev seemed quite content to let her establish the schedule, responding to her gentle bullying with satisfying gratitude. Dutifully he obeyed her injunction to avoid overdoing it in the sun and acceded to her choice of chicken with peanut sauce for lunch. She also made sure he consumed invigorating tea at the morning break and several scones which were served at three in the afternoon.

In between these times she obtained a deck of cards and played gin rummy with her recuperating patient. And all the while the conversation flowed easily between them. Dev talked about his adventures as a travel agent, and she told him about the small pleasures of running a bookshop in a quaint Victorian fishing town.

"We have something in common," he observed at one point as she beat him for the third time at gin rummy. "Both of us know what it is to be struggling small-business people."

The thought of a similarity in their careers pleased Tabitha and her normally small, private smile widened into something approaching brilliance. Dev stared at her for a moment as if he'd lost track of his thoughts. Then he appeared to remember what he had been about to say.

"Listen," he went on earnestly, "just because I'm not up to having a swim, don't let me keep you out of the pool. It's getting quite warm out here, and I'm sure you want to cool off a little."

Tabitha's eyes widened in dismay. "Oh no, I'm fine, really, I am. I'm enjoying the warmth." Have this man see her in a bathing suit? Not a chance!

Now why should she feel so awkward at the thought? she asked herself grimly. She'd been swimming before in the cruise ship's pool, heedless of what poolside opinion might be. But she was accustomed to receiving only mild glances that quickly slid off and went on to more interesting targets. In her demure bathing suit, with its small skirt at the hips, she felt she achieved a certain anonymity amid the bevy of sleek maillots and bikinis. This afternoon, however, simply because they had spent so much time together and had gotten to know each other, Dev was bound to give her more than a brief, disinterested once-over glance if she were to change into a swimsuit. She'd certainly give him more than a quick look if he were to change!

"Go on, Tabby," he encouraged. "I'll just stretch out here on the lounger and rest a bit while you cool off. Everyone else is in the pool!"

"I don't…well, that is…" She fumbled to a halt. There really wasn't a whole lot she could use for an excuse. And she didn't want to make him think she was self-conscious about the prospect of having him see her in the suit. Besides, he was a gentleman and a friend. He wouldn't be judging her against the other women, would he? Dev Colter was too intrinsically gracious to stoop to that sort of masculine cruelty. "All right, if you're sure you don't mind being deserted for a while, I'll go downstairs and change. Be right back."

She was shy, Dev thought, hiding his amusement as he watched her hurry off toward the staircase which led to the lower decks. Was she really embarrassed at the thought of flaunting that nicely rounded body in a skimpy little swimsuit? He liked the small, growing signs of awareness he was seeing in her. The notion of having her aware of him as a man was satisfying. Still, he cautioned himself, he had to go slowly. The desire to pounce on her was increasing every hour he spent in her company but instinct told him it would be disastrous. Better to have her relaxed and open, slipping over the edge into sensual awareness before she quite realized what was happening.

Dev settled back in his lounger, wincing as he jolted a few still-healing muscles. Then his mouth tilted upward faintly at the corners as he closed his eyes and waited for the return of his tabby cat. He felt rather like a medieval hunter setting out to capture an unfamiliar creature described in a bestiary. The knowledge that he was deliberately setting lures and baiting traps took him by surprise. What was it about this woman that made him want to keep her near? Was it just that he was luxuriating in the soft comfort she offered? Probably. It was a rare treat.

Women in his life tended to fall into one of two categories. They were either lethally dangerous or else they were cute, sexy creatures who found him temporarily fascinating because of his past. He made a determined effort to avoid both varieties. Unfortunately, there didn't seem to be a whole lot of choice in between the two extremes. Or perhaps, up until recently, he hadn't realized what he was missing. How did a man know to go looking for something when he wasn't fully aware that it existed?

Tabitha emerged on deck twenty minutes later swathed in a huge, oversized towel. She smiled a little uncertainly as she came toward him, hugging the towel closely. Conscious of his role, Dev returned the smile, keeping the greeting light and totally unthreatening. He wanted the tabby purring comfortably.

"Here, I'll hold your towel for you while you go in the pool." Casually he held up his hand, making it nearly impossible for her to avoid complying. It took her a couple of seconds but then, apparently deciding she was being ridiculous, she let the towel unwind and handed it to him with a brave nonchalance that made him want to chuckle indulgently.

"I'll be right back," she assured him, turning at once toward the pool. He watched as she first sat down on the edge and then slid into the water. It was a hell of a swimsuit, he decided dryly. He hooked his arms around his knees, sitting up to watch as Tabitha dutifully began swimming laps. The suit was black with tiny little nondescript flowers scattered about. High-necked, with wide straps and a little skirt designed to help conceal the roundness of her hips, the garment stood out amid the gaily colored bikinis and maillots simply because it was so utterly different! He wondered if she realized that in seeking anonymity she had unknowingly made herself somewhat unique on the sun deck of the ship.

Even though it had been designed to conceal rather than reveal, there was only so much a swimsuit, any swimsuit, could cover however, and Dev found himself thoroughly enjoying the sight of Tabitha as she gamely went back and forth in the pool. She was so soft looking, he thought wonderingly. Soft and gentle and feminine. He remembered the touch of her hand on his forehead the night before and took a deep breath. A determined man might resort to violence to obtain that kind of softness for his very own.

And he'd sure as hell resorted to violence for less reason than that in the past!

But violence wasn't the way with a woman like this. He narrowed his eyes against the sun as Tabitha emerged, dripping, from the pool. He watched the way she shook back her warm-colored hair and then he realized he wasn't the only one whose eyes were following the progress of the staid little swimsuit. With instinctive male alertness he pinpointed the one or two other knowing masculine gazes, and he frowned in unaccustomed displeasure.

Almost simultaneously he realized something else.

Tabitha was totally unaware of the other eyes on her. It wasn't a casual pretence of unawareness inspired by feminine self-confidence but a genuine lack of consciousness that she was attractive. It was as if she simply didn't believe herself the type of woman to draw a second glance from any man. Perhaps it was that very lack of sensual response on her part which made the other masculine gazes slide on past to other swimsuits.

But none of these other men had nearly gotten themselves killed in a back alley on some scroungy Caribbean island and then had this woman come to their rescue. Nor had they discovered the warmth and gentleness in her touch as Dev had the previous night. He decided he preferred to keep the information to himself.

"I've been thinking about tonight," Tabitha began hesitantly as she neared Dev's lounger and quickly picked up the towel he extended. As soon as she got it wrapped around her she felt instantly more comfortable. His gaze had remained politely on her face as she approached, and his smile was one of genuine welcome. Such a nice man. He neither leered nor ignored. Her eyes sparkled with enthusiasm as she took the seat beside him. "Are you going to feel up to having dinner in the main dining room?"

"I'm feeling better by the minute. And thanks to all the food you've been stuffing down me today, I think my energy level will be high enough to manage the exertion of dinner," he said, chuckling and leaning back against his folded arms.

"Oh good. Well, I was wondering about perhaps seeing the purser and getting your seat assignment changed. There's an empty place at my table and as long as you're not traveling with anyone else…?'' She tried not to chew on her lower lip as she waited for his reaction. He had been so amenable to every other suggestion she'd made today that when this idea had come to her in the pool, she had decided to risk the potential rejection.

"I'd like that, Tabby," he murmured, closing his eyes against the glare of the sun. "I'd like that very much."

Tabitha's smile was very private this time as she leaned back to let the heat of the day finish drying her body. Her self-confidence soared. Dev wanted to have dinner with her. She was suddenly enormously glad she'd taken the initiative. Perhaps he'd been wondering how to do it, himself, but hadn't wanted to seem too demanding of her time. Dev Colter wasn't the kind of man who would want to push himself into a woman's company unless he was sure she wanted him to do so, she thought smugly.

That smug feeling was still with her as she entered the dining room on Dev's arm that evening. Dressed in a gauzy, free-floating, white dress trimmed in turquoise at the hem and throat, she felt light and delicate beside his solid strength. He was wearing a dark, linen sports jacket over tan trousers, and the ebony cane in his hand seemed to lend an air of dignified restraint to the total picture of lean, conservative masculinity. Best of all he acted as if she were the only woman in the whole room.

"You look very charming tonight, Tabby," he murmured as they took their seats. "I only wish I could ask you to go dancing later on."

She glanced up in surprise and confusion. "Oh, will you be too tired, do you think?" she asked weakly. She had been hoping the evening would extend well beyond the dinner hour. The tinge of disappointment was almost painful.

He gave her an odd glance as he picked up his menu. "Not too tired. But I'm afraid I don't dance." His silver glance slid sideways to the cane hooked on the back of his chair.

Relief flooded through her. "Good grief, is that all you're worried about?"

"Well, it does rather limit my capabilities on the dance floor," he drawled a bit coolly.

"So who wants to dance? I'm not really a very good dancer anyway. We'll sit at one of the little tables and drink gin and tonics and make brilliantly perceptive observations about all the other people on the dance floor." She chuckled.

Dev studied her for a moment. He seemed about to ask a question but shelved it as the others who had been assigned to their table began to arrive. The conversation quickly became general. The two other couples, both in their mid-fifties, had heard of the affair on St. Regis and were full of interested concern as they discovered themselves seated next to the victim. Somewhat to Tabitha's surprise, Dev seemed quite willing to talk about it although he chose to emphasize her own part in the matter.

"Believe me, I was never so glad to see anyone in my life as I was Miss Graham here when she came around the corner," he announced feelingly.

"Not quite true," Tabitha heard herself retort. "You said that if I were the U.S. cavalry, I was a bit late, as I recall!'' She turned to the others, astonishing herself with her willingness to make a joke of the whole thing. ''It was one complaint after another, you know. First that I was late and then that I wouldn't let him pour an entire bottle of rum down his throat in the taxi on the way to the boat and later, when he asked for a bowl of soup, that I showed up with a full-course meal. There's no pleasing some men!''

Dev contrived to look hurt. ''Well, I really could have used the rest of that bottle of rum the taxi driver offered!''

One of the other men at the table laughed loudly. ''I don't blame you, Colter. Sounds like good medicine to me!'' He picked up his whiskey sour and swallowed thirstily.

It wasn't until Dev had escorted Tabitha to a seat in the elegant cocktail lounge after dinner that he asked the question she had seen in his eyes just before the meal.

''Why don't you dance?'' he inquired blandly as he ordered drinks.

Tabitha lifted one shoulder dismissingly. ''Not enough practice, I suppose. It takes a fair amount of experience to feel confident on the floor, you know.''

His mouth twisted. ''To tell you the truth I wasn't much good even before my accident. Now the cane gives me the perfect excuse to stay safely seated.''

''Your accident?'' she began delicately, aware of an avid curiosity.

''Umm.'' He nodded unhelpfully and then, instead of responding to her unasked question, he went on with another of his own. ''So why haven't you acquired much practice, Tabby? Don't they date in that little Victorian village where you have your book-shop?''

She smiled. "Definitely. We're not *that* antiquated. But since my marriage ended, I haven't gotten out a great deal." She bit her lip. "Actually, I didn't get out a great deal before my marriage. Or during it, to be perfectly precise."

He gave her an odd glance. "When were you mar-ried?''

"A couple of years ago. It didn't last long, I'm afraid. Only about a year."

"What happened?" Dev asked.

"I guess you could say it was cancelled due to lack of interest," she tried to retort brightly, but a flash of remembered humiliation came and went briefly in her eyes.

"Which of you lost interest in the other?"

She eyed him with the first, faint trace of wariness she had yet experienced around him. "Are you sure you want to discuss this particular subject?"

He smiled with a reassuring gentleness that im-mediately relaxed her. "It's probably a case of failure loving company. My ex-wife lost interest in me right after my accident."

"Oh!" Tabitha exclaimed, her heart going out to him at once at hearing the bold statement. "I didn't realize... Well, I know exactly how you feel. It's rather demoralizing, to say the least, isn't it?"

"When your mate loses interest? To say the least," he agreed dryly. Then he went on with warm assur-ance. "I can't see anyone losing interest in you, though, Tabby."

Her smile flickered brilliantly at the compliment

and then faded into a self-mocking grimace. "Actually, the surprise was that Greg married me in the first place. I was the kind of girl who made a fortune baby-sitting in high school because I never had a date. In college I was the sort who always got her term papers done early, because I had plenty of free evenings to study. Later I made a success of my little bookshop, because I had plenty of time to devote to it. When Greg came along, I was as astonished as everyone else was when he asked me to marry him! I hadn't exactly been besieged with offers."

"What happened, Tabby?" The silver eyes pinned her intently.

She shrugged. "What I didn't understand at the time and what he didn't bother to tell me was that he had moved into town in an effort to recover from a blazing love affair which had gone wrong. I guess I seemed like a quiet, undemanding sort of female who didn't remind him in the least of his lost love. It was a classic case of marrying on the rebound and it proved a disaster. I knew almost immediately that I was never going to be able to satisfy him, and when I found out he was always comparing me with the great love of his life, I realized it was all pretty hopeless. He realized it, too. And then his dream woman came back into his life. That resolved the situation rather quickly. Greg and I were divorced almost at once."

"And he went back to his blazing love affair?"

"Yes. It was all for the best. But the experience didn't improve my ability on the dance floor," she concluded in an attempt at flippancy. Then, very bravely, she asked, "What about you, Dev? Did your wife really leave you because of your accident?'' Her eyes were dark with sympathy.

He shrugged, glancing down at his drink, and then raised his gaze once more to her concerned face. ''The marriage had been disintegrating long before the accident. I hadn't proved to be what she wanted in a husband. I suppose my lifestyle sounded more exciting to her than it really is. Or perhaps I sounded more exciting to her than I really am,'' he confided dryly. ''People sometimes think that if you're well traveled, you're a jet-setter type. And I'm not, to put it mildly. I'm just a hard-working businessman. It took me quite a while to recover from my accident, and by the time I had, we had decided to go our separate ways. She found someone else before the divorce was finalized.''

''We seem to have several things in common,'' Tabitha observed softly.

He looked at her and then he smiled. ''We do, don't we?'' There was another short silence and then he added in an even quieter tone, ''You don't bore me in the slightest, Tabby.''

''That's the nice thing about a shipboard romance, isn't it?'' she said without stopping to think. ''By the time boredom sets in, the boat is back in port and everyone can go his or her own way.'' Almost instantly she wished her tongue would dissolve in her mouth. Lord! Now he was going to think she was suggesting that he have a shipboard affair with her! And she hadn't meant that at all. Had she?

But Dev appeared not to have picked up on the awful ramifications of her words. Instead he only smiled benignly and glanced around at the dancers

who were beginning to crowd the floor. "How many
of these people do you suppose are only involved in
shipboard romances?" he asked easily. "I'll take the
first guess. I'll bet that couple over there in the far
corner is having an affair."

Grateful for the diversion, she played the game
with him. "How can you tell?"

"Look at the way they're all wrapped up in each
other."

"Maybe they're newlyweds."

"No rings."

"Hmm. You're very observant," she said, rather
surprised he had been able to pick up such a small
detail from such a distance across a dark room.

"I have good eyes." He shrugged, as if it were an
unimportant fact about himself he had long since
taken for granted. "Good ears, too."

"Better than normal?" she asked, firmly resisting
the impulse to make a Little-Red-Riding-Hood-style
comment. He had clearly intended no humor in the
remarks.

"So I've been told," he confirmed idly. "Your
turn."

"Okay, I'll choose that couple near the bar. I'll bet
they're involved in an affair, too."

"Nah. They're married."

Tabitha frowned. "Rings?"

"Yeah, but that's not what gives them away. Look
how he keeps glancing over his wife's shoulder at the
blonde by the window. He's flirting like hell."

"You sound very knowledgeable," she accused.

"I'm a man. I understand my own sex," Dev
growled.

"And married men always flirt?"

"That one does. Let's see, who else can we find?"

"This could make an interesting parlor game," Tabitha murmured, getting into the spirit of the thing.

Two hours slipped past and Tabitha realized she was enjoying herself with unaccustomed abandon. She even allowed herself more than her usual two drinks and was beginning to feel quite bubbly. It was probably the alcohol in part, but she knew that she was high on something besides the unaccustomed number of drinks. She was enthralled with the relationship that was blossoming between Dev Colter and herself.

"You look very happy," he observed as they ambled out on deck to drink in some of the moonlight and the sea air. Actually it was Tabitha who ambled. Dev still moved with a great deal of stiffness. Even when he was healed, he would be less than agile with that left leg of his, Tabitha thought compassionately. He would still be vulnerable. Her expression softened dreamily at the thought.

"I am," she said simply. "I've had a lovely evening." An unfamiliar self-confidence was welling up in her as she leaned against the rail and clung lightly to his arm. "I can only think of one more thing that would make it perfect." For a second her heart almost stopped as the words left her mouth. Surely this wasn't Tabitha Graham talking?

Dev looked down at her, his hard face shadowed in the moonlight. Only his silver eyes seemed light and reflective. "What's that, Tabby?"

She took a deep breath and then, with a fragile sureness which was entirely new to her, she lifted her

face and raised her hands to splay against the front
of his jacket.

"Would you mind very much if I kissed you good
night?" she asked politely.

Three

"It's all right," she murmured with a reassuring smile when he said nothing in response to her inquiry. "I'm really quite harmless. Tabby cats are, you know."

"I'm not so sure about that," Dev said quietly. "But the appearance of being harmless and gentle is probably part of your charm. I wouldn't mind at all if you kissed me good night. But I should warn you that it's been a long time since I said good night to a woman under moonlight. In fact, it feels like it's been forever."

Tabitha lifted sensitive fingers to touch the side of his hard cheek, her eyes like sherry wine as they revealed her sympathy. He seemed so very vulnerable physically and now, she sensed, he was also vulnerable emotionally. "Has it, Dev?"

He inclined his head once, a little shortly, and she

had the distinct impression that he was embarrassed about his lack of sophisticated experience. Then he leaned against the railing and hooked the ebony cane over the metal beside him. "I've spent a lot of time alone since Amanda left. Too much, it seems, if you have to be the one to ask me whether or not you can kiss me. I should have swept you off your feet with a romantic assault out here on deck," he concluded wryly as he softly folded his large hand over her fingers, which still rested lightly on his chest.

Instinctively Tabitha moved a little closer, her face lifted anxiously. "Don't be ridiculous, Dev. If you had tried to stage a grand assault, I would have wondered what in the world was going on. It wouldn't have been in character for you at all!"

"No?"

She shook her head firmly. "Dev, you're special precisely because you're not like other men. You're sensitive and, I think, a little shy. Just like me. I feel comfortable with you. Don't you understand? Men always seem to be playing some sort of macho game and you don't do that. You're honest and gentle and you don't try to flirt with every beautiful woman who walks past. You and I are friends. We have things in common. All of that is so much nicer than having to worry about playing a game, don't you think? It's because I feel we're on the same wavelength that I felt comfortable asking if I could kiss you."

"And if I'd assaulted you instead?" he asked half-humorously, silver eyes gleaming.

She laughed up at him, the amusement mirrored in her warm gaze. "I would have thought you probably had too much to drink. I'm not the kind of woman men assault, but more importantly, you're not the kind of man who goes around pouncing on women.''

His gaze narrowed slightly. "Are you sure that doesn't make me a little dull?''

"It makes you wonderful," she whispered happily and stood on tiptoe. Her fingers went lightly around the back of his head as she raised her lips to brush them against his mouth.

That flower-soft caress was truly all she had intended. A part of Tabitha, sensitized by the intriguing new relationship which was developing between herself and the man she had rescued, had simply wanted a touch of intimacy. Something in her had wanted to deepen the closeness just a bit. Or perhaps it was merely a desire to broaden the spectrum of the friendship being established.

Whatever the basis of the impulse, Tabitha knew she mustn't go too far with it or Dev would wonder what had gotten into her. She didn't want to frighten him off by demanding more than he was prepared to give. No, she had planned to limit the kiss to just a brief gesture of affection.

What she hadn't counted on was the unexpected warmth of his mouth against hers, nor the faint tremor in his hand, which still enclosed her fingers. She withdrew until there was an inch or so between her lips and his, but she stayed on her toes and her hand at the back of his head did not move.

"Again?" she heard herself ask huskily.

"Please." His voice was even huskier.

Very carefully she leaned against him this time, finding a distinct pleasure in the feel of his hard chest against her full breasts. When she moved her mouth lightly against his, he muttered her name and the sound of it was strangely intoxicating.

"Tabby. Sweet Tabby."

Almost imperceptibly his fingers tightened around her hand, pressing it against his jacket. Then she was aware that his other hand was settling ever so hesitantly at her waist, resting on the curve of her hip. He was just as nervous and uncertain about all this as she was, Tabitha thought wonderingly. Perhaps it would be easier for her if she took the initiative. A vulnerable, sensitive man like this would be anxious not to press matters farther than she wished them to go.

Relaxing into the role of the one who must set the pace, she felt a little more of her weight rest against his solid frame. He seemed so substantial, so strong, absorbing her lighter weight with ease. If she hadn't already learned of the other side of his nature, she might have been nervous about the strength in him. But she did know of his sensitivity and his vulnerability, and so she let herself enjoy the delicate moment.

It was strange being the one who sampled and tasted and set the boundaries. There was a curious freedom in it, unlike anything else she had ever known before. There was no painful agony of suspense, wondering whether or not she would attract or bore her partner. There was no nervousness about how far to let the situation go. Instead she experienced a heady sense of excitement.

His dark hair seemed crisp and inviting to the touch and her fingers began to move a little awkwardly in it. She felt another tremor pass through his body and her own anticipation increased. He wasn't bored, she thought exultantly. Her touch was eliciting a response in him; she could feel it!

The moment when her mouth parted invitingly beneath his passed without her actually being aware of it. One instant there was a barrier between their tongues and the next she was tasting the inside of him.

She heard someone moan softly and realized belatedly that it was herself. The next shiver she sensed was one which flowed through her body, not his. Her feeling of anticipation was elevated by several quantum leaps, sending her senses into an unfamiliar whirl.

For an endless moment she explored the intimate taste of him, unaware that her nails were sinking delicately into the back of his neck. He was taking most of her weight now as he leaned against the railing and somehow his legs had spread apart. She was standing cradled between his thighs and the heat of him passed easily through the thin gauze of her dress. He was so warm and inviting, so undemanding, yet welcoming.

She was becoming hungry, Tabitha realized distantly; even a bit greedy. The urge to learn more intimate details of his body was rapidly deepening. She mustn't scare him off, she reminded herself. She didn't want to do anything that would spoil the unfolding relationship.

His tongue played with hers as she caressed the inside of his mouth with exquisite care and it followed as she led the way back into her own mouth. Once she had him inside, she moaned softly again, inviting him to explore as he would.

For some reason his legs seemed to tighten around hers and the strong hand at her waist dropped lower on her hip, kneading gently. But mostly Tabitha was aware of the incredible thoroughness with which he used his tongue. She was becoming captivated by what she had found. The blossoming sensuality she was experiencing was totally new to her. Above all she must not push it.

"Tabby?" he rasped a little thickly as she reluctantly withdrew her mouth from his.

"It's all right, Dev," she mumbled a little unsteadily. "I know things are moving too fast. Don't worry, I won't let them get out of hand."

"Tabby," he began carefully, as though searching for difficult words. "Tabby, I..."

"Don't," she pleaded, stopping his mouth with her fingertips. Her eyes smiled warmly up at him. "Don't say it. I know this is taking both of us by surprise. I wouldn't dream of spoiling it by rushing things. I expect it's the moonlight and the wine. Neither of us is too accustomed to romance, apparently!" Her curving lips invited him to laugh with her at the situation in which they found themselves.

Dev stared down at her for a long moment, silver eyes opaque. "I, for one, am not very familiar with it at all," he finally murmured.

"I know. That's one of the things I like so much about you," she told him honestly.

"You do?"

"Umm. I feel like I'm dealing with someone I understand. Someone who has the same reservations and concerns I do. The same fears."

"What fears?" he questioned deeply, apparently

having a little difficulty in swallowing. Poor man. Was he so very nervous of her?

"About building something meaningful between two people; about wanting to be certain there's real depth in a relationship before committing yourself to it. Oh, Dev, I feel I know you so well!" Tabitha exclaimed in satisfaction. "We have so much in common. I know neither of us wants a casual fling. It's no wonder we don't fit into this crowd on board. We're both a couple of misfits, aren't we?"

"In a way." He sounded almost cautious as he intently studied her upturned face. "I have to admit that neither of us seems quite what the cruise line had in mind in the way of potential passengers when it printed up the brochures! I'm on board for obvious business reasons. What made you buy a ticket, Tabby?"

"Fantasy, I think," she told him whimsically. "I had this image of what a Caribbean cruise would be like, you see. Balmy nights and sunny days filled with exotic color and excitement. Maybe I thought I would become a different person on board, I don't know. All I do know is that after I'd been on the ship one day, I realized I was the same old me and ten days at sea wasn't going to change things."

"Would you really want to be different? Even for ten days?" Dev asked in a gently neutral tone.

"I think every woman who thinks herself rather average has fantasies occasionally about becoming a femme fatale, about living a romantic adventure. Don't men have personal fantasies about being someone different?"

The question seemed to take him back for a moment. An unreadable expression flitted across his face and then he said slowly, "They do. I'd be lying if I said they didn't. There have been times lately when I've wished I was another kind of man."

"Oh, no," Tabitha interrupted with conviction. "Don't wish that! I wouldn't want you any different."

"You like the man I am?"

"Very much." She touched her fingertips to the lines at the side of his mouth, automatically soothing the uncertainty she sensed in him. "I like the man you are very much, Dev Colter. I wouldn't change a thing."

He gave a sideways glance at the ebony walking stick slung over the rail. "Not even the cane?"

She smiled at that. "The only reason I might be willing to see that changed is because of the pain your accident must have caused you. Other than that, no, I wouldn't particularly want to see it changed, if you want the truth. It gives you a distinguished air, like the gray in your hair."

"Thanks!" he muttered wryly. "The gray is a sign of being nearly forty, Tabitha."

Tabitha lifted her fingertips from the lines at his mouth to the flecks of silver in his deep brown hair. "I love the gray in your hair. Like moonlight caught in the shadows."

"I think you've been reading too much fantasy, but I won't complain," he groaned. Both of his hands had settled on her waist now, and she still stood between his thighs. "So here we are, two people who would like to live a fantasy and en route we've found something else, hmm?"

"That's a nice way of putting it," she whispered. It seemed to Tabitha that his fingers curved with a small amount of force into the curve of her hip. Or perhaps it was simply her imagination.

"Tabby, if this is reality, I think I prefer it to a romantic adventure on the high seas," Dev said huskily.

Her breath caught in her throat as her mind spun with all the potential implications of what he was saying. "So do I, Dev. I've thoroughly enjoyed this evening. I only wish you weren't still recovering from that awful incident on St. Regis."

"I feel much better," he assured her quickly.

"You don't have to pretend with me." She chuckled. "I'm the one who saw you in that alley, remember? I know very well you must still be hurting in any number of spots! And it's undoubtedly time you were in bed. You know what the doctor said, lots of rest."

Aware of where her duty lay, Tabitha stepped back out of his arms and took his hand in hers. Deliberately she started toward the entrance to the lower decks.

"Are you going to tuck me in tonight, Tabby?" Dev asked as he obediently followed.

She tried to analyze his tone, wondering if he sounded hopeful or was simply making a small joke. Then it occurred to her that his head might be aching. Perhaps he was obliquely asking her for another massage. "Have you got a headache?"

"No, I don't," he answered automatically and then blinked as she looked back at him inquiringly. His voice trailed off abruptly as if he had said something he wished he hadn't. Then he essayed a crooked little smile. "But it was very pleasant having you stay with me last night until I fell asleep."

"No one likes to suffer alone." She smiled as they headed down the long corridor lined with stateroom doors. "I was very happy to stay with you." At least he seemed to think she had left him after he'd fallen asleep. It was nice to have that confirmed. It made everything so much more comfortable between them. She looked up as they arrived at her cabin door. "Well, good night, Dev. I hope you sleep well."

"I'll call you before breakfast in the morning," he said deliberately. Then he added quickly, "That is, if you'd like to have breakfast together?"

She took pity on his suddenly anxious expression. "I'll look forward to it." Then, feeling very confident about what her reception would be, Tabitha balanced herself again on her toes and brushed her mouth lightly against his. "See you in the morning," she said before he had a chance to react. She stepped inside her own cabin and closed the door. Her own aggressiveness was enough of a shock to herself. No point in alarming him with it, too!

Out in the corridor, Dev watched the stateroom door shut firmly in his face and his knuckles whitened around the curved handle of his cane. Damn it to hell! This was taking more out of him than he had expected. How much patience did she think a man had?

With another muttered oath he started on down the corridor to his own room. There were only five days left on the stupid cruise. Five days left to figure out how to let Miss Tabitha Graham talk herself into bed with him. Well, he shouldn't complain, he told himself as he opened the door to his cabin. Look at the progress he'd made this evening. He'd made himself seem so nice and safe that she'd actually taken the initiative out on deck. And to think he'd spent the previous hour in the cocktail lounge wondering how to go about taking her into his arms without scaring the daylights out of her!

But it had all worked out very nicely, even if she had cut him off far too quickly. Dev shut the door behind him and set down the ebony cane. Tabitha was going to find herself in his bed eventually. He just had to be patient. You couldn't stalk a tabby cat with an elephant gun. Subtlety was called for here.

It was strange, he decided as he caught sight of the grim set of his face in the mirror, he would never have thought himself the subtle type. But then, he'd never tried to attract a woman like Tabitha Graham, either. A man was never too old to learn new tricks, it seemed. Then he winced as he sat down on the edge of the bed, his fingers going to his bruised ribs.

He might not be too old to learn new tricks in some areas, but there was no doubt that he was too old to be dabbling in his former line of work. How in hell had he ever let Delaney talk him into making that pickup on St. Regis?

Painfully, wishing he had another bottle of whiskey handy, Dev undressed and got into bed. It was really much more pleasant when Tabitha was around to fuss over him. He shouldn't have automatically denied the headache. Unfortunately he had spoken without thinking, and by the time he'd realized his tactical error it was too late. If he'd just thought it out beforehand, he could have had her here right now using her wonderful fingertips on his forehead.

Muttering about his failure to think fast enough on his feet, he reached out to switch off the bedside light. Then he lay staring out at the moonlit darkness beyond the window.

There was no point kidding himself. Tabitha had no idea at all of the kind of man he was. She had given him a fantasy role. To her he was gentle and vulnerable and sensitive. Just the kind of man she wanted. If he kept his head and didn't make any serious errors during the next couple of day, she would crawl into his lap like a trusting little cat. And then he would find out exactly what it took to make her purr.

With that thought in mind, Dev closed his eyes and went to sleep. He did not stay awake long enough to ask himself just why it was so important to make Tabby purr.

The ship's itinerary the following day included an afternoon stop at another of the lesser-known islands on the list detailed in the brochure. Tabitha was looking forward to it with great anticipation. She bubbled over at breakfast as she read the description given in the ship's daily newsletter.

"It says here that a lot of expatriate-artist types have established a colony on the western tip of the island and that passengers from the ship are welcome to visit," she informed Dev over fresh papaya.

"I take it you'd like to visit the colony?"

"Definitely! No telling what sort of unusual things might be going on there."

"I'll bet." He chuckled.

"I meant in the way of creativity," she told him repressively.

"So did I. Put a bunch of free-spirited artists together on an island, and there's no telling what sort of creative endeavors they'll get up to."

"You're teasing me," she accused, but the knowledge left her feeling remarkably light-hearted. It was the sign of a good relationship when each party felt free to gently tease the other, wasn't it?

"You're right. I'll look forward to seeing the colony as much as you will," he assured her blandly. "Another cup of coffee?"

"Please." Then Tabitha frowned. "Are you sure you're feeling up to the trip? How are your ribs this morning?"

"A little sore, but nothing that should stop me from accompanying you."

And they didn't, apparently. Tabitha double-checked several times during the afternoon to make certain Dev wasn't overexerting himself, but he seemed able to maintain the pace she set. Together they toured the small shop at the art colony, and Tabitha fell in love with one item after another. A wide variety of work was being done in all sorts of media from woodworking to pottery and weaving.

"Look at this lovely dragon design, Dev," she exclaimed jubilantly as she examined a woven wall hanging. "He's going to look great over my fireplace."

Dev eyed the hanging thoughtfully. "He does appear to be looking for a home. Look at those pathetically pleading eyes. Too bad about the big teeth and the fiery tongue. Who'd want to take a chance on him as a house pet?''

''Don't be ridiculous! I would! He's gorgeous.'' She began rolling up the hanging. ''And a perfect copy of a small German bronze figure I have.''

''How did dragons make their way into bestiaries? From fairy tales?''

''The monks weren't that naive,'' she sniffed. ''They knew the difference between fairy tales and real life. No, they probably came from descriptions of large serpents like pythons. And there are some other big reptiles in the world which could have been described as dragons. When you think about it, it's not hard to imagine some real-life dragons.''

''Well, if you're going to take him home, I'd very much like to buy him for you,'' Dev said. ''To replace the little carving that got left behind on St. Regis.''

''Oh, that's okay. You needn't do that,'' she said hurriedly, pleased at the offer.

''I'd very much like to, though, Tabby. Will you let me?''

She cocked her head to one side at the soft note of entreaty in his low voice, and then she gave him a dazzling smile of acceptance. He really wanted to do this. How could she refuse? A man like Dev Colter would feel guilty at the knowledge that he'd been the cause of her leaving her trinkets behind on St. Regis. Such a thoughtful person!

''That's very kind of you, Dev. If you're quite sure you want to do this...''

''I am.''

She lifted a shoulder in helpless appreciation.

"Then thanks. I'll think of you every time I look at him," she added with a grin.

"What is it about him that's going to remind you of me? The fiery breath or the nasty-looking tail?"

"I think it's the eyes," she said musingly and then blushed as she realized it was the truth. Brilliant silver pools filled with a barely masked vulnerability. That was what she saw when she looked into Dev's eyes.

That night she again floated into dinner on his arm, and it seemed to Tabitha that her conversation had never been so witty and intelligent. The evening drifted past on dragon's wings, full of magic and shimmering excitement. Dev must have felt some of the sorcery, because he seemed as wrapped up in her as she was in him. Everywhere she led, he followed, willingly changing conversational directions, duplicating her order of turbot with cucumber sauce at dinner and insisting that she choose the wine.

So enthralled was she in the warm, vibrant relationship which seemed to be developing that Tabitha was unaware of the increasingly frequent glances she was receiving from more than one nearby male passenger. Her animation and sparkling excitement were like small, glittering lures that frequently caught the attention of others. But after so many years of playing the role of observer rather than participant, Tabitha was not equipped now to recognize that kind of subtle masculine attention.

Dev, on the other hand, discovered he'd developed a whole new set of instincts where Tabitha Graham was concerned. Sitting across from her in the cocktail lounge later he saw disaster approaching long before it walked over to the table. He did some quick evaluation of the situation even as Tabby began a detailed discussion of basilisks.

"That's the creature that supposedly kills with only a glance," she was saying chattily as Dev watched a rugged, athletic-looking, blond man start toward the table. "It could be a completely fabulous creature with no basis in reality, but some people have pointed out that it could simply have been confused with some reptiles which can spit their venom. Those poor monks sitting around their tables dutifully writing out bestiaries had no way of verifying many of the reports they got about animals in far-off places, remember. At any rate, although any creature who looked straight at it reportedly keeled over, the thing was apparently vulnerable to weasels. That was the theory at the time."

Dev tried to produce a basilisk-style stare which he directed at the blond man who was now directly behind Tabitha. It had no effect, probably because the other male had eyes only for Tabby. He'd taken one glance at Dev's cane earlier in the evening and had undoubtedly concluded, quite accurately, that it limited the older man's social activities. And the band was a very good one that night. Dev knew Tabitha was about to be asked to dance.

"Excuse me," the man said with a smile that came straight off a California beach. "Would you care to dance?" Tabitha looked up in surprised confusion. Before she could respond, the stranger turned to Dev and went on coolly, "I'm sure you won't mind if I borrow her for a while, will you?" Left unspoken was the rest of the sentence but Dev heard it, anyway.

After all you can't ask her out on the floor. Why shouldn't I take her away from you?

The casual challenge had an unexpectedly savage effect on Dev. He was not normally the possessive type, and even if he had been, he knew Tabitha well enough by now to know she was hardly the kind of woman who would play two men off against each other even if she got the chance. Hell, Tabitha wouldn't know *how* to play that kind of game. But the knowledge didn't lessen his purely masculine reaction to the blond beach boy.

"I beg your pardon?" Tabitha was saying, glancing up at the stranger with a puzzled expression in her huge, sherry eyes.

"I asked if you'd like to dance. The name's Steve, by the way. Steve Waverly." The man gave her another of his sunny grins, confidence radiating from every pore. He had assessed Tabitha's companion and decided there was no threat from that quarter.

"Oh," Tabitha murmured, sounding rather flustered, but nonetheless pleased, "that's very kind of you, but I'm really not much of a dancer, I'm afraid. Not much practice, you see. And I was right in the middle of telling Dev, here, about basilisks. And weasels."

"Weasels?" The stranger's smile slipped a bit as he attempted to follow the conversation.

"You use weasels to get rid of basilisks," Tabitha explained kindly. "They might not actually have been weasels, of course. There is some speculation that they were mistaken for mongooses which do tackle snakes. And since basilisks may have been a type of snake, it makes sense that mongooses might…"

She was interrupted by a muffled groan from the other side of the table. Instantly her head came around in frowning concern. Dev gave her his bravest smile. "Sorry, honey. My ribs are acting up again. You know the doctor said they would be sore for a few days." He gingerly put a hand inside his jacket, testing the bruised ribs. "And I'm afraid all that exercise today might not have been the best thing for my leg. It's aching a little. But don't worry, I'll just take a couple of aspirin while you have a dance with Mr. Waverly. Maybe that and another couple of drinks will deaden the pain."

Instantly Tabitha was on her feet, Steve Waverly completely forgotten as she rounded the table to take Dev's arm. "You will not sit here and gulp aspirin and alcohol! Of all the silly notions. What you need is more bed rest. I should never have dragged you off to that artist's colony this afternoon. How could I have been so thoughtless? And now I've kept you up till all hours when you ought to be sleeping. Come along, Dev. I'm taking you back to your cabin right now!"

Dev allowed himself to be assisted to his feet, his fingers closing strongly around the handle of the cane as he smiled blandly at his puzzled foe. "If you'll excuse us, Steve?"

Tabitha seemed to remember Waverly's presence. "Oh, yes, please excuse us, Mr. Waverly," she said with a charming smile. "Dev is still recovering from a terrible incident back on St. Regis, you know. He needs plenty of bed rest. See you later," she added rather absently as she took Dev's arm and started him out of the cocktail lounge.

They had almost reached the door when Dev pulled back slightly. "Just a second, honey, I forgot to leave a tip. You wait here and I'll be right back."

"I could take the money back to the table," she began earnestly.

"No, that's all right. Won't take a second." He patted her hand reassuringly and turned back into the crowded lounge. Using the cane with a polite ruthlessness, he forged a path back through the dancers until he found the table Steve Waverly occupied alone. The younger man glanced up in astonishment as Dev approached.

"Listen, weasel," Dev drawled in chillingly polite tones that immediately got Waverly's complete attention. "I think we need to clarify a small matter here. Just so there's no misunderstandings, the lady is private property. Come near her again and I will take you apart piece by piece. There are plenty of other more exotic creatures on board this ship. Stay away from my tabby cat."

Waverly's handsome face went through a variety of expressions as he rapidly reassessed the situation. Dev was pleased with the final wariness which settled into the other man's blue eyes. He nodded in satisfaction, not feeling any compunction at all in having used nearly forty years of harsh experience and the resulting masculine assurance to quell his younger rival. Dev knew damn well he could be intimidating when he chose, and tonight he found himself choosing to be exactly that: thoroughly intimidating.

"Good night, Mr. Waverly," he murmured arrogantly, turning back toward the door with masterful confidence. Through the bobbing dancers he could just barely make out Tabitha's anxious gaze as she searched impatiently for him. Dev smiled to himself, quite pleased. He remembered to inject a hint of brave suffering into his smile as Tabitha caught sight of him and came forward to take his arm once more.

"Did you leave the tip?" she asked politely, guiding him out the door.

"I left a tip," he murmured in satisfaction.

"I'm sure it will be appreciated."

"I can only hope so."

"How's the leg?" Tabitha inquired as he leaned more heavily on her arm.

"It aches, I'm afraid," Dev admitted. It wasn't altogether a sham, either, unfortunately. The damn leg was hurting a bit tonight. And so were the ribs for that matter. Forty years might buy a man enough experience and confidence to intimidate younger rivals but they also brought some less pleasant rewards such as the aches and pains generated by all that accumulated experience.

The discomfort, however, was almost worth it just to see the warm concern in Tabby's eyes as she led him back to his room. Dev felt the gentleness of her touch on his arm and sensed the tenderness she wanted to extend. The evening was going very well, he decided. Very well, indeed.

"Is the leg hurting very badly?" she asked anxiously as he opened his cabin door.

"It's felt better," he told her grimly.

She chewed on her lower lip for a second. "Look, why don't you get into a bathrobe or something, and I'll massage it for you," she finally offered. "Would that help? And I can put a compress on your ribs, too, if you like.''

Dev sighed in satisfaction and tried to make it sound like a suppressed groan of pain. "That would be fantastic, Tabby. How can I thank you?" He leaned the ebony cane against the wall and steadied himself with a hand braced against the bathroom door. "I'll be right out as soon as I change," he told her calmly. He was proud of the casual tone of his voice, especially given the fact that his blood was starting to move with a heavy beat in his veins.

She was waiting for him when he emerged from the bathroom a few minutes later. He was dressed only in a beach towel that he had wrapped carelessly around his waist. He saw the way her wide eyes lingered on his bare chest before she quickly raised them to his face. "Sorry—" he smiled easily "—I don't have a robe.''

"I see. Well, lie down on the bed and let me at that leg. I'll get a cloth from the bath for your ribs, too," she said industriously, looking everywhere but at his half-naked body.

He sank heavily down onto the bed which she had already turned back for him and watched indulgently as she scurried around the room, collecting a warm damp cloth and her nerves. He liked the way his near nakedness had thrown her into awkward confusion. She was becoming increasingly aware of him, he realized. It was just a matter of time.

Carefully arranging the sheet so that it covered as much of him as possible, Tabitha eventually settled down to the task at hand. At the first touch of her gentle fingers Dev closed his eyes and exhaled slowly. It was going to be a toss-up, he decided, between the way she aroused him and the way she relaxed him. But he knew which sensation was going to carry the day. Already his body was tightening with awareness.

"That feels so good, Tabby," he growled as she worked on his aching leg. "Much better than aspirin."

"How did you hurt your leg, Dev?" she asked in a soft voice, as if afraid of intruding on his privacy, but unable to resist the question any longer.

"I had an accident a couple of years ago. Zigged when I should have zagged," he returned as nonchalantly as possible.

"A skiing accident?"

"No, uh, car accident," he corrected automatically. The story should be automatic by now. He'd told it enough times. "Got cut with some flying glass."

"Yes, I can see the scars," she whispered, tenderly kneading the area around the knee where the evidence of the accident still persisted. He heard the gentleness in her voice and smiled to himself. It was so nice to have her fussing over him like this. Who would have thought after all these years that he'd find himself wanting to immerse himself in a woman's tenderness? Having a female for an occasional bed partner had always seemed more than sufficient in the past.

It wasn't just her attention and compassion he was enjoying, Dev realized with a flash of honesty. He was also enjoying playing the role she had assigned him. He rather liked being the kind of man she admired. Tabby found him intelligent, a stimulating conversationalist, well traveled and very much the gentleman. With her he actually felt like a cultured, gracious businessman who was on a cruise for pleasure as well as business. God! She'd be utterly appalled if she knew what sort of tip he'd actually left behind in the cocktail lounge this evening!

But Waverly deserved what he'd gotten. Tabby was Dev's own private discovery and damned if he was going to let another man come along and steal her away just when he had her halfway into bed.

Actually, she was sitting on his bed right now. He felt her adjust the warm compress on his ribs.

"Any better?" she asked after a moment.

"Much. You're a natural nurse, Tabby. Probably missed your calling by going into the book business."

He kept his eyes closed, aware that her hands were fluttering a bit awkwardly on him now. She wanted to touch him more intimately, he realized, and she didn't quite know what kind of excuse to use to do so. Maybe he should pretend to fall asleep again. Last time she had stayed all night. If he could get her to lie down beside him tonight, he'd have it made, he was sure of it. Experimentally, he tried a yawn.

"You must be exhausted, Dev. Will you be able to sleep with your leg hurting?"

"It's not hurting nearly so much now," he told her in a voice that was rapidly thickening from something besides weariness. How much more of this was he going to be able to take? When would she realize how his body was reacting to her? Damn it, she'd been a married woman. Regardless of how lousy her husband had been in bed, she must know when a man was becoming aroused! Maybe he should just grab her.

Hell, he'd waited long enough, hadn't he? She was so close and he *knew* she was aware of him as a man.

But if he could just hold off a little while longer, she'd take the initiative, and he wouldn't have to risk spoiling her image of him as a shy, vulnerable gentleman. His hand clenched under the sheet. How much longer?

Dev sensed Tabitha's increased agitation. Her own sensual awareness was there in her touch now. He could hear her increased rate of breathing and even though he steadfastly kept his eyes closed he had a mental image of what the action was doing to her lovely breasts. Her rounded thigh was pressed against his as she sat beside him on the bed, and it was all he could do to resist closing his hand over the intriguing curve.

When she leaned over him to adjust the sheet, he held his breath. Perhaps now. Last night she'd found the courage to kiss him good night. If she tried that again this evening, he would simply close his arms around her and pull her down onto the bed. His mind raced with the image of what he would do next. It would be easy to roll over on top of her, trapping her beneath him with one leg while he stifled her protests with a kiss.

No, he couldn't wait any longer. When she leaned down to kiss him good night, he'd risk losing his status of gentleman and grab her. Hell, a man couldn't wait forever.

"Good night, Dev. I'll see you in the morning for breakfast." Suddenly her hands had left him.

Dev's eyes snapped open in dismay as he realized there wasn't going to be any good night kiss. She was halfway out the door before he could think of anything to say and by then it was much too late. A second later the door closed solidly behind her.

"Damn it to hell!" he gritted, his clenched hand lifting to pound impotently into the pillow. "Damn it to hell and back! What went wrong?"

It seemed to him that his leg ached worse than ever.

Four

Tabitha knew exactly what had gone wrong. She'd lost her nerve at the crucial point and, since Dev was too shy and too sensitive to take the initiative, she had lost the opportunity. Damn!

Back in her cabin she paced the tiny floor space and wondered what would have happened if she'd let the massage turn into lovemaking. She was almost certain Dev wouldn't have rejected her. It had seemed as though his body had grown tighter, harder, under her hands instead of more relaxed, and there could be only one reason for that. She had managed to arouse him, she was sure of it. Poor man. He must wonder at her intentions!

In all honesty, what were her intentions? She certainly had not set out to seduce Dev this evening. Her immediate concern had been his bruised ribs and aching leg.

But somewhere along the line she had realized what was happening to both of them. And she'd lost her nerve.

The knowledge of their mutual attraction had shaken her far more than she would have expected. After all, she had been a married woman! Still, the lessons she'd learned from a husband who had found her boring had been drilled into her so well that it was difficult to escape them. It was difficult to be sure that she had at last found a man who found her interesting.

He was like her in so many ways, she thought. Perhaps, in a way, he was even more withdrawn and vulnerable. After all, in addition to his unhappy marriage, he'd also suffered that terrible car accident. She'd seen how aloof and distant he'd held himself during the first few days of the voyage, never mixing with the other passengers.

Yes, he was even more cautious than she was when it came to relationships, Tabitha decided, and that meant that it was up to her to keep the wonderful association developing.

In other words, if there was to be any hope for something meaningful between Dev Colter and herself, she was going to have to take the initiative and seduce him. He was simply too uncertain, too vulnerable to do it on his own.

Deliberately seduce a man? She, who had never been given any reason to think herself either sensual or irresistible? Whose husband had made it very clear that she was a nonentity in bed?

But Dev Colter was not her husband. He was as different from Greg as night from day. Dev would not expect an acrobat in bed. And in spite of his physical weight and strength, Tabitha just knew Dev would be a tender and infinitely gentle lover. Perhaps even a lover who could let her find out for herself if there was any hope of releasing a sensual side to her nature—a fantasy side.

"Face it, woman," she lectured herself in front of the mirror. "You're falling in love with the man. And you were the one who said she'd never get involved in a shipboard romance!"

Could she let this marvelous man just disappear from her life without making some effort to cement a more permanent bond between them?

What would have happened if she'd obeyed her impulse to touch him more and more intimately tonight? What if she had tried another kiss? Would he have responded? Dealing with a basically shy male had its advantages, but it also had a few drawbacks, she decided ruefully. It left her with the task of making the final decision.

There were only a few days left on this trip. So little time left. If she was going to do anything substantial, it would have to be soon. Resolutely, Tabitha lifted her chin and eyed her reflection. Damn it, she was falling in love, *really* falling in love for the first time in her life. Was she going to let her natural hesitation and shyness ruin her one chance?

But set out to deliberately seduce a man?

With a groan of dismay Tabitha sank down onto her bed, chin in hand, and contemplated the enormity of what she wanted to do. On top of everything else there was the awful risk that she was misinterpreting things terribly. Perhaps Dev wasn't all that interested in her. Oh, God. How awful if she put him in an embarrassing and untenable position by trying to seduce him! *Mortifying!*

The alternative was to return to Port Townsend and go sedately back to work in her bookshop without ever having learned the truth about his feelings for her. She knew she would never forgive herself for her cowardice. Dragon-seducing was dangerous work, however. She didn't feel very well equipped to tackle the job. Tabitha groaned again and flopped back on the pillows, staring at the ceiling.

There was no repressing the excitement and the sense of wonder she experienced as she fell asleep considering the immediate future. It was as if her whole life were focused on a crucial turning point, leaving it up to her to choose the final path. Never, since the day she had decided to go into business for herself, had she felt quite so poised on the brink.

It took great courage to don the flowing, colorful caftan without first putting on a bra the next morning. Anxiously Tabitha stood in front of the mirror and eyed the effect. Wasn't she a little too well rounded and a little too old to be going without a bra? On the other hand the turquoise and red garment was so loose-fitting that Dev might not even notice the absence of a bra beneath the material!

The question was, would Dev be attracted to the sensual shape of her unconfined breasts even if he did notice? Fingers drumming on the counter, Tabitha hesitated. Maybe she looked better with the bra on. No, she didn't droop or anything and nearly every other woman on board dressed quite freely. With a brisk nod of decision, she decided to leave the bra off.

Feeling enormously daring and quite liberated, she ran a brush through the soft bell of her hair and located her sandals under the bed. She'd take things a step at a time. Breakfast without a bra came first.

The knock on her door came just as she was lacing up her sandals. She took a deep breath and went to answer it with her most casual smile.

"Good morning, Tabby," Dev began calmly as she opened the door. "I came to see if you were ready for breakfast." As if he had been standing in the room ten minutes earlier, watching her dress, his silver eyes flicked down, sweeping across the bodice of the caftan.

"I'm starving," Tabitha said, hurriedly stepping out into the corridor before she lost her nerve. Oh, lord! He'd noticed. She was absolutely sure of it. So what was his reaction! "How are you feeling this morning?" she remembered to ask.

"Quite refreshed," he drawled, taking her arm in a grip that seemed more intimate than usual. Did the back of his hand always come into contact with the side of her breast when he took her arm or was she just more conscious of the warmth this morning because there was one less barrier? "I always seem to sleep well after you've tucked me into bed," he went on lightly.

He seemed to be waiting for something. She sensed the hesitation in him and all at once understood it. He was wondering whether or not to kiss her good morning. Feeling more confident because she'd had good luck with the action before, Tabitha smiled and braced herself lightly against his shoulder with one hand. Then she brushed his mouth with the most fleeting of kisses.

"I'm glad," she murmured.

"That I sleep well after you've put me to bed? So am I." As she eased back down he lowered his head and returned the kiss. This time the contact held longer and there was a warmth to it that lingered long after Dev broke the kiss.

The greeting signaled the start of the day, and the sunny hours rolled past with a sensation of rapidly coalescing intimacy. Dev seemed more than willing to be led down the primrose path, Tabitha decided in wry humor as she stretched out beside him on a pool lounger. He might be shy but he was not disinterested!

"Do you feel up to a little swimming this afternoon?" she asked conversationally as he sat down beside her. They had both changed into swimsuits, and she found her glance wandering toward the curling mat of hair that formed a large triangle on his chest. Apparently he had removed his bandages, and more than once she had to drag her eyes away from the spot where the tip of the triangle disappeared into his trim swimsuit.

"I think so. How do the bruises look?" He glanced down at his ribs, more or less giving her free license to do the same.

"Much better," she managed with an air of briskness. God, he was hard. Hard and lean and wonderfully sleek. She wanted an excuse to touch him, any excuse. "A little black and blue still, but definitely healing," she went on, extending her fingers to the line of his battered ribs. His skin was warm from the sun. He glanced up, his silver eyes meshing with hers, and she forgot to withdraw her hand.

Without a word he covered her hand with his own, pressing it briefly against his chest, and then he released it to get to his feet. "Last one in buys the drinks tonight," he announced cheerfully. He began moving the few feet to the pool's edge without the aid of his cane, the limp very pronounced. It certainly didn't totally incapacitate him, however!

"Hey!" Tabitha exclaimed, realizing she was being left behind. "No fair. I didn't get any warning." She dove in about two seconds behind him, surfacing a moment later to find him laughing down at her. "For a supposedly wounded man with a definite limp, you move awfully fast," she accused.

"A man will do a lot when the provocation is sufficient. For a tabby cat, you seem to take fairly well to water."

"I still think we should run that race again. I deserve a head start, being the weaker sex and all!"

"I wouldn't dream of setting back all the progress made by the women's movement."

She grinned. "That's very noble of you. Try this bit of progress on for size!" Taking him by surprise, she managed to push him over backward in the water. He went under very nicely. But he managed to circle her wrists with his own, and she found herself following him below the surface.

For an instant the world was transformed in the abruptly silent, watery environment. Tabitha couldn't resist. Taking her courage in both hands, she let herself float down until her body lay along his and then, eyes tightly closed, she kissed the strong line of his throat. His hands seemed to wind themselves into her hair, holding her head in place, and she felt her legs tangle excitingly with his. It was a moment of magic and undeniable passion.

The magic ran out at the same instant as the air in Tabitha's lungs. Realizing she was about to try breathing water, she kicked reluctantly free and surged to the surface. Automatically her eyes scanned the faces of the nearest sunbathers.

"Worried that someone may have noticed?" Dev asked softly as he came up beside her. "Don't fret about it. They'll think you're a mermaid."

Tabitha blinked water out of her eyes. "Dangerous creatures, mermaids," she managed to say lightly, striking out for the side of the pool. She hoped no one had noticed that little scene but it was hard to tell. She still wasn't accustomed to this seduction business!

"Why are they dangerous?" Dev asked, trailing beside her in the water.

"Sailors who hear their calls at sea and follow them are never heard from again," she told him in dark tones. "They lure men to disaster."

"I thought the ladies who lured sailors to their deaths were the Sirens," he protested laughingly.

She liked his laughter, Tabitha decided. She liked it very, very much. "Well, there's some confusion between Sirens and mermaids in the various bestiaries. You can't blame the scribes for getting them confused. All they were really sure of was that you had to be damn careful of the creatures. In fact, there are a lot of general cautions about women thrown into the texts. The female of the species is often rather dangerous, I'm afraid. Or at least the medieval people thought so.'' She smiled brilliantly.

"You know how men are about learning from history,'' Dev rasped softly. "They have a bad habit of forgetting the lessons of the past no matter how many times they're repeated.''

Tabitha drew in her breath, a wave of excitement coursing through her. "Meaning you're going to turn a deaf ear to all those warnings about Sirens and mermaids and Harpies?''

"Meaning I don't think I have anything to fear from a tabby cat,'' he corrected, silver eyes gleaming in the sunlight. "I'm not really dealing with a Siren or a mermaid, am I?''

She searched his face, uncertain of his real message. "No,'' Tabitha had to admit. "Probably not. But you said yourself that to a man who's never seen a tabby cat, she might seem very unusual.''

"She does,'' he told her whimsically. "Unusual and charming and very appealing.''

"But not dangerous?''

"I'm not sure yet.''

Tabitha treaded water, staring up at him for a moment longer. Then she made up her mind. Not dangerous, hmm? Delicately she grasped his slick shoulders, letting herself slide closer. He didn't move as she closed the distance between them. Probably thought she was going to kiss him again, Tabitha decided mischievously. He was getting to like her kisses, she knew.

Very deliberately she bent her head and sank her teeth lightly into his bare shoulder.

"Ouch!" Startled, he drew back.

Tabitha didn't let him go. She smiled blandly up at him. "I've decided I don't like being labeled as 'not dangerous.'"

He eyed her a little warily. "I see. I, uh, won't make the mistake again."

"Good." She released him to swim to the side of the pool again. "Hungry? It's almost time for tea and scones." She had him properly confused now, Tabitha decided gleefully, even somewhat intrigued. She hadn't missed the speculative light which had gleamed for a moment in his eyes. This certainly was a delicate game, this business of seducing a man. You had to be so careful not to go too far and scare the victim, yet you couldn't be too hesitant or nothing would be accomplished!

It was as they left the dining room and headed toward one of the lounges on board that Tabitha reminded herself of the two staples of sophisticated seduction: alcohol and verbal innuendoes.

Matters had been proceeding very nicely up to this point, she decided, vividly aware of the feel of Dev's hand on her back. He had been finding one excuse after another to touch her all evening, and she had been encouraging the contact. The dress she had on was a swirly, little thing, loose but also of quite thin cotton in a vibrant, coral shade. Her bra had once again been left behind in her stateroom. She was very conscious of the lack of it when the evening breeze on deck plastered the coral cotton against the length of her body.

The overall effect was a bit more than she had intended, Tabitha realized as she saw her escort's eyes drop almost lazily to the outline of her breasts. Fortunately they soon entered the darkened cocktail lounge and during the process of finding a table, Tabitha recovered her composure.

Alcohol and innuendoes. Booze and sexy conversation.

She would get Dev Colter just a bit tipsy, she decided judiciously. Enough to lower some of his natural, gentlemanly reserve. And then she would talk about sex.

"Don't forget I'm buying the drinks this evening," she said cheerfully as they sat down. "Even though I have definite qualms about the manner in which the race at the pool was conducted, I *did* lose. Never let it be said I'm not noble in defeat!" She smiled up at the approaching steward. "We'll have two gin and tonics. Doubles."

"Doubles?" the steward repeated politely.

"Doubles," she said firmly and then turned the smile on a rather watchful Dev. Now for the titillating conversation. She took a deep breath and widened her smile. "Did I ever tell you how interested the scribes who wrote the bestiaries were in the, uh, mating habits of the various animals?"

He blinked. His long, dark lashes lowered briefly and then lifted to reveal a politely interested silver gaze. "No, I don't believe you did. A subject of great interest, hmmm?"

Tabitha cleared her throat. She had started this and she was damn well not going to falter now. As soon as the drinks arrived she launched into her lecture on the sex habits of medieval animals. "They thought elephants extremely modest, you know. So chaste that an elephant couple had to chew on a bit of mandrake in order to overcome their natural shyness about sex.''

''Mandrake?''

''Ummm. I guess the scribes thought it served as an aphrodisiac.''

''Rather like a modern-day couple having a few drinks before testing each other's inclinations?'' Dev suggested in mild interest.

She peered at him a little sharply and then relaxed. He seemed genuinely interested in the discussion. ''Well, yes, as a matter of fact. I guess that is a good parallel.'' She groped for another piece of information. ''They thought that the virility of a horse was hampered if you cut its mane,'' she continued brightly.

''Something to keep in mind next time I go to the barber.''

Tabitha frowned for an instant, trying to decide whether or not he was joking. ''The texts don't draw any lessons for human males on the matter,'' she told him dryly.

''I see. What other interesting facts have you gleaned from the bestiaries?'' Dev sipped his drink, watching her expectantly.

''Well, vultures, it seems, don't go in for sex,'' she confided smilingly.

''No sex?''

''It was thought that lady vultures just gave birth whenever the notion struck them.'' That didn't sound very sexy. What else could she remember? ''They thought vipers had a particularly violent method of propagation. After mating, the female viper bit off the male's head.''

"Do you mind if I have another drink? This discussion is getting somewhat gruesome."

Tabitha straightened and signaled to the steward. "Heavens, no. I'll get it for you. I'm still paying off my loser's debt, remember? We'll have two more," she instructed the steward.

"Doubles again, ma'am?"

"Yes, please." Tabitha went back to her lecture. "Where was I?"

"The female viper was biting off the male's head, I think," Dev reminded her gently.

"Oh, yes. Well, if it's any comfort, the monks writing the bestiaries didn't approve of such activity. They drew a few sharp lessons from it and passed them along for the, er, edification of human females."

"What sort of lessons?"

Tabitha experienced a moment of awkwardness which she overcame with another sip from her drink. Then she leaned forward and lowered her voice very meaningfully. "They strongly advised human wives not to resist the approaches of their husbands."

"In other words, not to plead a headache?" The silver gaze gleamed.

Tabitha nodded. "Here's your drink. Might as well take advantage of the fact that I'm buying, hadn't you?"

"Might as well." He downed a healthy swallow and waited for the next bit of bestiary lore.

"They thought partridges did it a bit too often. The birds were thought to be very sexually aggressive, constantly trying to mate. So much so that they often wore themselves out, poor birds."

"Fascinating."

"Lions were strongly approved of because they were thought to be loyal to their mates," Tabitha went on chattily. "There's not much information on the mating habits of dragons and unicorns, though. No one really knew too much about them, it seems."

"Perhaps it's just as well."

"You're probably right," she agreed thoughtfully. "Some things are better left to the imagination. Would you like another drink?"

"I haven't had a chance to finish this one," Dev pointed out politely.

"Oh. Well, perhaps in a few minutes."

"Thank you. You're very generous in paying off your debt." His mouth kicked upward at the corners.

She smiled brightly. "I try."

"Do you lose often?"

"Actually, no. I don't get involved in many contests," she explained with a chuckle.

"A non-participant?"

"Since kindergarten, I'm afraid. How about you? Were you the kind who went out for the team? Or did you tend to keep to yourself?"

"I've never been much of a joiner or a team player," he admitted. There was a small silence and then he held out his empty glass. "I'm ready for the next drink."

"I'll order you a surprise this time. Something a little different." They had so much in common, Tabitha thought blissfully as she selected a Tequila Sunrise for her escort. So very much. Did he see it, too?

"The entire evening is turning out to be one surprise after another," Dev drawled as the steward departed once more with an order.

"And we're only halfway through it," she retorted. But the sense of mounting excitement rippling through her was already making her head spin. Everything was going wonderfully on course. Dev showed every indication of being more than mildly interested in following her sensual lead. All she had to do was keep matters moving in the right direction and not lose her nerve in the process.

Gamely she plied Dev with drinks, watching hopefully for signs of relaxed inhibitions. She went back to anecdotes about the mating habits of animals from the bestiaries, and somehow the conversation seemed to keep its sensual orientation without much effort. There was nothing overt about the innuendoes, naturally. Dev wasn't the sort of man who would embarrass her with blatantly sexual remarks, unlike some men who had imbibed several drinks. But somehow everything seemed to be overlaid with a touch of sensuality.

Perhaps it was simply the combination of her mood and the balmy Caribbean night. By the time they left the cocktail lounge, Tabitha felt she had the situation completely in hand. Dev was, in fact, eating out of her palm. She had the heady realization that she could do just about anything she liked with him just then.

"Are you tired?" she asked, deliberately resting her head on his shoulder as they came to a halt by the rail. She let her arm wind around his waist.

"No," he murmured in her hair. "As a matter of fact, I feel much better tonight than I have since St. Regis."

"Not even a headache? How's your leg?"

"My head and my leg are fine, thank you."

"I see." There went the obvious excuses for guiding him downstairs to his cabin. She would have to try something more direct. "Aren't you feeling even a little tipsy from all those drinks I ordered for you?"

"Pleasantly high would describe the sensation." His breath gently fanned her hair as she snuggled closer.

'You don't want to lie down or anything?"

"I hadn't thought about taking a rest. Didn't feel I needed one."

"Dev," she said, lifting her head with sudden resolve, "I don't think I got around to telling you about the mating habits of tabby cats this evening."

She felt him go very still. Tabitha, herself, could hardly move now that she'd made her most suggestive play yet.

"No," he finally said, his voice sounding rather muffled, "I don't believe you did. How would you describe them?"

"Right now, I think it's fair to say they could be described as quite…quite *wanton*." Tabitha turned in his arms and circled his waist with both hands. Then she lifted her face in the moonlight, inviting his kiss.

Five

Tabitha saw the silver flame of desire in Dev's eyes as he obediently lowered his head and she knew she had won. She had succeeded in seducing him. The knowledge bloomed in her like wildfire, sending small shivers down her spine and making her senses tingle. She had actually made him want her!

As his mouth closed over hers she crushed her breasts against the hard planes of his chest, hoping he would thrill to the contact as much as she did. The husky groan from deep in his throat told her he was surgingly aware of her now.

"Oh, Dev," she whispered, lifting her fingers to twine them in his hair. "Tell me you want me just a little. Please tell me. I want you so much...."

"How could I resist you, tabby cat?" he muttered hoarsely as she nibbled suggestively on his lower lip. "So soft and warm and sweetly sexy." His arms closed more strongly around her, urging her closer.

Tabitha didn't hesitate. She buried her lips against his throat and let herself melt against his hardness. She was vaguely aware that he had hooked the cane over the railing and was leaning back, balancing both of them. Once again his legs had parted and she was between them, luxuriating in the intimacy of the embrace.

"A sleeping dragon," she murmured, her voice stirring with barely suppressed excitement. "I feel as if I'm waking a sleeping dragon."

"Do you see me as a beast, then?" he growled, gently dropping tiny kisses along the line of her shoulder.

"A fabulous beast. Gentle and strong and noble. A beast of legend."

"Tabby, Tabby, your imagination overwhelms me," he groaned. Dev's hands slipped down her spine to the contour of her hip.

"It's not my imagination. You are all those things. You're also shy and vulnerable and sensitive. The perfect man," she sighed. "And I've been wanting to make love to you all day. Will you mind very much?"

"Tabby, I'm yours tonight," he rasped thickly. "Take me and do what you will with me."

It was exactly the response for which she had been praying, but still Tabitha hesitated as a thought struck her. "Do you really mean that? It's not just the alcohol talking?"

"The alcohol?" He sounded as if he were only half-aware of the question.

"I've...I've been plying you with drinks all evening long," she explained in a burst of honesty that she instantly rued.

"You wanted me drunk?"

"I wanted you...*relaxed*," Tabitha corrected firmly.

"Ah, I understand. You used alcohol to lower my inhibitions and now you're worried I'll regret it all in the morning, is that it?" She couldn't tell what he was thinking. His voice sounded very muffled again as he put his lips to her wind-tossed hair.

"Will you, Dev?" Uncertainty flared for a brief moment.

She felt him shake his head. "No, sweetheart, I won't regret a thing. I know I shall wake up in the morning with wonderful memories of tonight."

"If you're quite sure..."

"I'm sure," he affirmed. Was that a hint of impatience she heard now in his voice?

Tabitha gathered her courage once more. "Well, then, would you like to come downstairs with me, Dev?" She pulled back, her hands still on his shoulders and searched his silvery gaze. The moonlight in his eyes made them mysterious pools which she couldn't fully delve, but there was no denying the passion she saw there. Wordlessly she lowered her hand, taking one of his in a gentle grip.

Dev followed silently as she led him toward the stateroom decks. All the way down the long corridor to her room she was pulsingly aware of his heavy, dark presence. Pushing aside the qualms and uncertainties she ought to be experiencing, Tabitha reminded herself that she was following her heart tonight. There was no need for fear or nervousness. If she gave in to either, Dev would leave in an instant, she was certain. He would do nothing to frighten her.

No, she decided as she unlocked her cabin door. This was what she wanted.

"Tabby?" Her name was a question as she resolutely closed the door behind him and she came close to touch his arm reassuringly.

"It's all right, Dev. I know what I'm doing."

"Do you?" he asked obliquely, his hands settling on her shoulders as she smiled tremulously up at him.

"Yes, Dev, I do. I want you. I...I care for you very much. I've been hoping all day long that you feel the same."

"How could I not want you?" he said simply, letting his fingers trail through her hair in slow wonder. "Oh, God, Tabby!"

She opened her mouth beneath his, inviting him inside and responding intensely when he accepted the invitation. She was falling in love with this man. There could be absolutely no doubt now. No one else had ever reached her in quite the same way, and she had never felt this flickering enchantment with any other man. Dev Colter was truly a fabulous beast: a silver-eyed dragon waiting for her to awaken him fully.

Slowly, with infinite care, she slipped her hands inside his jacket and pushed it off his shoulders. The garment fell to the floor. The feel of his smoothly muscled shoulders held her attention for a long moment as she tasted his tongue in her mouth, and then she began the unsteady task of unbuttoning his white shirt and unknotting the striped tie he wore.

Undressing Dev Colter proved to be a most satisfying endeavor. This was the first time she had been totally free to explore his body, and Tabitha found herself fascinated. It wasn't only the feel of his firm contours that aroused and intrigued her, it was also the utterly masculine scent of him, tinged as it was with aftershave and soap. And then there was the crisp, curling cloud of chest hair which drew her coral-tipped nails like a magnet. Wonderingly she let her thumbs glide across his flat, male nipples.

"Tabby, you're going to drive me out of my head tonight," he grated feelingly. She was aware that his fingers were trembling slightly as they found the zipper of her dress, and the knowledge warmed her. Poor Dev. He was so uncertain and nervous, so anxious to please. Tabitha was touched even as she allowed freer rein to her own passion.

When the dress fell at last in a wave at her feet, Dev drew in his breath as her full, round breasts came into view. For a moment Tabitha felt a shaft of unease, and then she saw the glowing appreciation in his eyes as he scanned her gentle figure and she relaxed. He found her pleasing, she thought triumphantly.

Wearing only the satin triangle of her underpants, she pressed herself closely against him and snuggled languidly when his palms cupped the curves of her derriere. She felt the strength of his fingers as he clenched them excitingly into her flesh. Tabitha trembled.

"Dev, I've never felt quite like this before," she confessed, letting her lips sample the flavor of his skin. "When I'm with you I feel marvelous. Passionate and exciting and sensuous."

"That's because you are passionate and exciting and sensuous." He slid his hands up her waist until they hovered just under the weight of her breasts. Then he let his thumbs gently rasp the nipples.

"Oh!" Instantly the tiny buds responded, forming hard, tight buttons of desire. Tabitha moaned, her eyes closing as she swayed more heavily against him.

"You make me feel exactly the same way," he confided deeply, holding her close.

"You don't mind that I'm seducing you tonight?" She smiled against his shoulder, confident now of her welcome.

"I can't even think straight at the moment. How could I mind what you do to me? Take me to bed, Tabby, please!"

She nipped erotically at his shoulder as she found the buckle of his belt and unfastened it. In another moment he was dressed as she was, in only his briefs.

"You're wonderful," she breathed in blatant admiration as she stepped back to drink her fill of his hard, muscular frame. "Sleek and strong and wonderful! Oh, Dev!" Moving forward again, she arched herself fluidly into his warmth, her fingers digging deeply into the coiled muscles of his back.

Somehow they were moving, shifting backward the few steps to the bed, and then Tabitha sank down, drawing him after her. Dev followed urgently, willingly giving himself up to her gentle touch.

Inflamed now with the sensual success she was achieving, Tabitha pushed imperiously until he fell onto his back. Dev watched with a lambent flame in his eyes as she knelt beside him and began to explore the sleek hardness of his body.

"Tabby, you must be a Siren or a mermaid. Anytime you call, I'll come. I could never resist." He gasped as she lightly scored the inside of his thigh with her nails and then he sighed as she sprinkled hungry kisses down his chest to the pit of his stomach. Her growing love for him was eliciting a surprising inventiveness from her, she realized. Never had she experienced such an overwhelming urge to explore a man's body.

Lost in a world of passionate discovery, Tabitha barely heard his muttered words. She listened only for the harsh sound of his heavy breathing and the gasps of desire which told her that whatever she was doing was right. His strong thighs twisted as she caressed him, and the thrusting evidence of his desire was hard and eager when she found it with her tender fingers.

"My yes, Tabby!" Then he seemed to lose control, pulling at her until she sprawled along the length of him in a silken tangle. "Now, honey, take me, now!" he blazed fiercely. His fingers went at once to the bit of satin at her hips, jerking it down over her full buttocks. Obediently Tabitha kicked the little garment free and then she came back to him.

Impulsively she settled astride his hips. *It would be like riding a dragon,* she thought fleetingly. And then, as his hands guided her firmly down onto him, she tensed, aware that he was far, far different from her ex-husband and in more than just a mental or emotional way.

"Dev?" The breath stilled in her throat as he waited, poised beneath her. She sensed the restrained power in him and for the first time, Tabitha hesitated.

"Are you suddenly afraid of me, Tabby?" he demanded softly, not trying to force her to complete the union. "You know I won't hurt you. Come close and make sweet love to me, little cat."

Then, his hands grasping the satiny contours of her thighs, he eased her down. Tabitha gasped as he filled her slowly and completely with his hardness. The shock of the union was unexpected. Her nails dug into his arms as she braced herself against the heavy impact he had made on her body.

As if he understood that she needed a moment to adjust to him, Dev held himself still beneath her, his hand soothing and coaxing on her thighs. She heard the fiery string of sensual words that he uttered in a dark, persuasive voice, and the combination of his tone and his touch made her body relax once more.

"That's it, honey," he growled as she slowly returned to the erotically reckless state she had been in only a moment earlier. "That's my tabby cat. Come and purr for me, sweetheart. Don't be afraid of me. You see how well we fit together? I would never hurt you. Just relax and love me. Let me lose myself in you. Just relax, honey."

The hypnotic words had the desired effect and as her body accepted his completely, Tabby forgot the shock of the intrusion. Besides, inside her now all was glittering, swirling fire. The heavy strength of him, which had momentarily intimidated her, was now a source of unbelievable excitement. She gave herself up to it with an abandon she had never known before.

Like riding a dragon.

The ride was infinitely more exhilarating than she could possibly have imagined. In her wildest fantasies, Tabitha had never thought herself capable of this thrilling response. Her body soared and spun, locked with his until the distant goal beckoned so urgently she could no longer turn aside. Caught in the slipstream which carried them both, Tabitha heard herself cry out, felt her body tauten in mindless tension, and then came a shivering release that left her weak and breathless.

Even as the sound of Dev's name left her lips, she was aware of him thrusting with even greater force than before and then he, too, was calling out. His voice was a thick, impeded shout of satisfaction that was wholly masculine and utterly timeless.

Playing the patient, sensitive gentleman definitely had its own rewards, Dev decided with languid, lazy pleasure as he came slowly out of the long aftermath of lovemaking. Countless rewards. Intensely gratifying rewards. He had gauged Tabitha Graham to perfection. She had climbed right into his lap just as if she knew where she belonged. He would bear the small marks of her claws with great satisfaction, remembering the passion which had incited her to leave the little nail marks on his shoulders.

Never had he allowed himself to be so sweetly seduced. His mouth curved with wicked delight as he lay with one arm around Tabitha and waited for her to stir. He had loved it, every minute of it, from the moment this morning when he had made the tantalizing discovery that she had deliberately failed to put on a bra, right up to the part where she had plied him with liquor and lectured him about the mating habits of animals. Fantastic. He would remember this night as long as he lived. If only there were more time left on the cruise! The thought of turning Tabby loose in a few days was very unpleasant.

He would have to do something about that. Nobody but a fool would let someone like Tabitha Graham walk out of his life. He'd never met anyone like her, and he had a fairly good idea he wasn't likely to run into anyone similar again. There had to be some way of ensuring that she would be around to seduce him again and again. And one of these days, when she was no longer shy of him, he would return the favor in full measure!

He was contemplating just how he would go about that task when Dev saw her lashes flutter. Lazily he propped himself on his elbow and stared down at her.

"You can't hide forever, Tabby. Open your eyes and look at me, sweetheart."

Her lashes lifted and wide sherry eyes regarded him with something between trepidation and hope. Dev leaned down and kissed the tip of her nose.

"I wasn't hiding," she protested carefully. "I was just sleepy."

He smiled. "Sure you're not feeling shy?"

"Maybe. A little."

"Not used to seducing men, hmm?"

"Well, no, now that you mention it," she retorted gamely. But he was right. She did feel shy and wary and rather unsettled. He looked happy and contented, though. Wonderingly she traced a path along the line of his perspiration-damp ribs. The bruises were still quite visible. "Are you all right?" she asked. "Nothing hurts?"

He grinned and Tabitha swallowed under the impact of the expression. "Nothing hurts. Nothing at all. I feel fantastic. How about you?"

"I, well, to tell you the truth, it was a...a very interesting experience," she told him, her eyes going to the level of his chest.

"A very interesting experience!" he echoed, sounding slightly taken aback. "What on earth does that mean?"

"It means I've never felt anything quite like what just happened," she admitted candidly. "I...I told you my husband found me boring. Well, I'm afraid I found him a little, er, boring, too. You see, he didn't have much patience with me, and I guess I wasn't a very warm sort of wife or something." She coughed a bit awkwardly and pressed on. "At any rate, I've never...that is I hadn't experienced the full...I mean..." She floundered to a stop and raised her eyes pleadingly. "You know what I mean."

"Ah, Tabby," he groaned softly, "you amaze me. How could anyone as sweet and warm and loving as you are have gotten this far in life without learning the full extent of your own passion?"

"I don't think anyone has ever thought me particularly passionate before," she said very honestly. "I've never even thought of myself as passionate. I've never really been able to let myself go before. But with you I feel free somehow. Free and brave and even sexy. Oh, Dev, I think it's because we're so much alike, you and I," she continued earnestly. "Don't you feel it, too?"

"I think I understand you perfectly," he murmured.

"You didn't mind being seduced tonight?" she

asked hopefully, eyes brimming with her feelings. She was in love. There could be absolutely no doubt now. Never had she felt like this.

"I loved being seduced tonight. In fact, I was going to ask you if you felt like seducing me all over again?"

"Again?" She looked up at him in astonishment. *Again?* After what they had just been through?

"I wouldn't dream of demanding too much of you," he began quickly as he saw the clear hesitation in her. His tone was humble and very anxious. "You've been more than generous tonight. I should go back to my cabin now so that you can get some sleep. After all, a woman like you would probably appreciate some privacy now. I don't mean to invade your life and force myself on you...."

"I don't mind," she interrupted quite bluntly. "I don't mind at all." Smiling invitingly, she put her arms around his neck and pulled him down to her. Dev needed no second urging.

Tabitha awoke the next morning with the feeling that her whole world had changed during the night. The knowledge brought with it a disorienting mixture of anticipation and uncertainty, pleasure and shyness.

For a long, private time she contented herself with simply gazing at the sprawled form of the man sleeping beside her, noting every detail with eyes that revealed her new-found love. How could she have been so incredibly lucky? Who would have thought that this cruise would bring her a man like him? He was so perfect, so absolutely perfect for her that it was almost frightening. She was old enough to know that life seldom offered such ideal relationships.

What if Dev didn't feel the same way about her?

What if he grew bored as her husband had grown bored?

What if he was only interested in a short-term affair?

No! He wasn't the kind of man who would have allowed the situation to develop as far as it had if he didn't feel as involved and committed as she did. Dev Colter was too much like herself to do that. Whatever else happened, she would always be certain that his feelings for her during the night had been genuine and deep. Determinedly she pushed back the covers and slipped out of bed, heading for the bath.

Of course she *had* been guilty of rushing things last night, she chided herself in the shower. There was no way she could deny the fact that she had set out to seduce the poor man and had succeeded.

The thought of herself as a seductress gave her a certain gleeful excitement, but it also brought with it uncertainty. What if she had pushed Dev a little too quickly? What if she'd hurried him into a physical commitment before he was quite ready? Perhaps she shouldn't have taken the initiative. Would he be resentful of her efforts this morning in the clear light of day? She was frowning over that notion when the shower curtain was pushed aside.

"Good morning," Dev said gently, silver eyes raking her worried expression. He smiled. "I had the feeling you might be in here berating yourself for being such a charming Siren last night." His eyes were warm, roving over her wet, nude body with remembered pleasure. "Having second thoughts?"

"A...a few," she admitted, vividly aware of his nakedness as well as her own. Under the force of the hot water she could feel her skin turn pink from the tips of her breasts to her earlobes. She buried her face industriously in a washcloth. "I mean, only if you are," she mumbled into the cloth. "I shouldn't have rushed you, Dev. Perhaps you weren't ready for that."

"If I seemed less than ready last night, I sincerely apologize," he drawled meaningfully.

Tabitha went redder than ever. "You know I wasn't referring to your...your..."

"Sexual prowess?" he interposed politely.

Was he teasing her? Or did he think she might have found him disappointing last night? That possibility made her lower the washcloth. She swung anxious eyes to his. "Oh, Dev. You were perfect last night," she breathed.

He stepped into the shower and circled her waist with large hands. "So were you," he told her simply. Bending his head, he kissed her forehead. "Stop worrying. You'll never get anywhere as a seductress if you get into the habit of having second thoughts the next morning!"

Her mouth curved tremulously. "Seductresses shouldn't have consciences?"

"Nope. But it's obvious you do, don't you?"

"I rushed you last night."

"I enjoyed being rushed."

"You're quite sure?"

"I'm positive," he murmured, nibbling appreciatively at her neck.

She relaxed and the smile on her lips curved a bit wider, lighting her sherry-colored eyes. "Well, if you're not going to gnash your teeth in dismay and ask how I could have been so callous as to get you drunk and then take advantage of you..."

"I'm not."

"Then I suppose I shall just have to ignore my qualms, hmm?"

"As long as you don't ignore me," he agreed. Dev caught her hand and spread her fingers across his chest.

"I'd never do that," she assured him earnestly.

"I think I'm going to hold you to that promise." He found her wet mouth with his own as Tabitha eagerly leaned into his strength.

By the time they had finished breakfast the ship had dropped anchor in the harbor of yet another of the out-of-the-way islands on its itinerary. Once again Tabitha had done her research.

"What's this one got to offer?" Dev asked, peering doubtfully toward shore as the tender boat carried them toward the dock.

"You ought to know, you're supposed to be checking it out for your clients, remember?" she chuckled.

"Somehow all these islands are beginning to seem alike."

"A fine attitude for a tourist agent!" She examined the brochure in her lap, the sea breeze ruffling her hair as she bent over the colorful paper. "It says not to miss the gardens of the secluded old hotel on the hill to the east of the town. Apparently they were designed by a famous English landscape artist some-time during the last century for a plantation owner. The plantation went under and has since become a hotel patronized only by the elite.''

"And now us. There goes the neighborhood," Dev sighed. "I've heard of the place, though. Three hundred dollars a day for a room. Haven't been able to talk many clients into trying it lately."

"Well, the gardens are said to be spectacular. There's even a maze! That should be fun."

"Thinking of abandoning your lover somewhere in it and leaving him to wander helplessly forever?''

Tabitha jerked her head up in astonishment, struck by the hint of something other than teasing buried in his voice. Was he genuinely worried that she wasn't feeling as committed this morning as he was? He was so very vulnerable, she thought with love. "Never," she vowed a bit gruffly. She could hardly say more. They were already docking.

Dev nodded, apparently satisfied, and took her hand to help her off the boat. Somehow, even with the necessity of wielding the cane, he accomplished the task with a kind of formal grace that made Tabitha feel cherished. His strength more than compensated for his limp, she realized. This morning, dressed in familiar khaki slacks and a shirt with the cuffs rolled up on his forearms, he seemed very vital and over-whelmingly masculine to her. Every time she looked at him she remembered what making love to him had been like and the recollections, she feared, showed in her eyes.

The day, which had begun so brightly, began to take a curious turn for the worse shortly after she and

Dev arrived by cab at the elegant former plantation home.

It was nothing she could put her finger on at first, merely a sense that Dev's mood had begun to undergo a subtle change. She noticed it first as they sat eating lunch in the dining room which looked out onto the beautiful formal gardens.

"Something wrong with the pear chutney?" she asked, watching as he toyed with the food on his plate.

He glanced up quickly and smiled. "No, of course not. Why do you ask?"

She shrugged. "You're not exactly wolfing down your food with your usual enthusiasm. Are your ribs hurting again?"

Was he being that obvious? Dev wondered as he denied the query. Or was it just that Tabby was so aware of him now that she was able to pick up on his moods very quickly? He would have to watch it or he'd ruin the whole day if he wasn't careful.

Still, there was no ignoring that uneasy sensation he'd experienced as soon as they had stepped out of the cab. Tabitha's enthusiasm had carried both of them up the grand steps and into the stately, open air lobby of the hotel before he'd had a chance to identify the prickly feeling.

But as soon as they'd sat down to lunch, Dev had realized the restless sensation wasn't going to disappear. It was intensifying. Two years was a long time to be out of the business, he thought, but some of the old instincts lingered apparently. The last time he'd experienced this disturbing feeling had been when he'd gone into that alley on St. Regis. Twice in one week didn't seem fair, not when he'd been free of the annoying habit for two years. Damn it to hell. Why had he agreed to get involved with Delaney again?

"Are you going to try the lemon syllabub?" Tabitha asked cheerfully, examining the dessert menu.

"That sounds good," he agreed promptly, not wanting to sound hesitant. She was already curious enough about his attitude. Deliberately he made himself eat the last of his curried lamb and rice, trying to appear enthusiastic. The excellent food was practically tasteless. He simply couldn't concentrate on it or enjoy it. What the hell was wrong?

There was nothing that could be wrong. Not here on this pleasant, sleepy little island in the Caribbean. Everything that had been wrong had already taken place on St. Regis. He should be clear of that by now.

But what if he wasn't? What if he'd unwittingly dragged Tabby into something connected with that mess? His fingers tightened around the wineglass before he carefully set it back down on the table. It was stupid to try to bury the prickly restlessness under a dose of alcohol. If there was trouble near, the last thing he needed was to be even a little under the influence when it hit.

The first priority was Tabby. In his thoughts that one conclusion leaped to the forefront immediately. Nothing else mattered as much as protecting her. She wasn't a target, of course, but being with him might make her one. Dev swore again, vastly annoyed with himself.

"Dev? Are you sure your ribs aren't hurting?"

He smiled a little, eyes softening as he absorbed the worried expression on her gentle face. It was rather pleasant having her worry about him. He was getting more than a little accustomed to the luxury. And maybe she was offering him the easiest excuse for cutting the day short. If she thought he was in pain, she'd rush him back to the ship, and that was beginning to look like the only way of erasing this uneasy chill down his spine.

"Well, to tell you the truth..." he began ruefully.

"I knew it!" she exclaimed, tossing down her napkin. "And you were going to play the macho role and pretend nothing was hurting, weren't you? Idiot! It's all my fault, too."

"Your fault?"

The red stain on her cheeks was delightful, he decided in amusement. "Because of last night," she mumbled, turning to search for the waiter.

"You're determined to go on some kind of guilt trip over last night, aren't you?" he teased her softly. "You woke up this morning berating yourself for seducing me, and now you're convinced you forced me to overexert myself. Stop worrying, honey. The ribs are just a little sore because I'm still recovering. That's all. Honest."

She was already madly signaling to the waiter, though, and it seemed simplest just to sit back and let her take charge of rescuing him again. She was so good at it, Dev decided in pleased satisfaction. Look at the way she ordered the waiter about. She was even abandoning her syllabub. Dev stifled a grin at what that sacrifice might signify. She eyed him critically as the waiter went off to prepare the check.

"I'm going to run to the rest room while he's getting the bill. I'll be right back, okay? Then we can

head for the ship. I think you should be lying down,"
she added with a crisp nod.

"I'm sorry to ruin the day like this," Dev said in
his most humble tones. It wasn't hard to fake the regret. He genuinely did regret spoiling her tour of the
island. But that nagging unease wasn't getting any
milder, and he'd learned long ago not to disregard it.
Probably a false alarm this time, but with Tabby
around he didn't intend to take chances.

"You're not ruining the day!" she assured him at
once, getting to her feet. "Now you just sit right here.
I'll be back in a minute."

He watched her go, thoroughly enjoying the way
her body moved beneath the light material of the red-
and-white-striped tunic she was wearing. The garment
was unbelted, naturally. All her clothes seemed light
and airy and unconfining. But somehow the very un-
defined line made her all the more provocative to his
eyes. And now that he knew exactly how beautifully
those breasts and that sweet rear curved, his imagination was quite capable of filling in details.

She disappeared down the long hall that led toward
the rest room facilities, and Dev turned his attention
back to collecting the check. The waiter was hurrying
across the room with it already, inspired, no doubt,
by Tabby's firm injunction. Dev tossed down a credit
card and then waited impatiently while the transaction
was completed. With any luck Tabby wouldn't daw-
dle in the rest room. At least she wasn't the kind of
female who felt compelled to repaint her face at every
opportunity.

He signed the credit slip and then glanced at his
watch. She'd been gone almost ten minutes now. How

long should he give her? She'd said she would be right back.

The gnawing unease grew. With a brusque movement Dev reached for his cane and got to his feet. The tension was getting to him, he thought. He wanted Tabby out of this place. False alarm or not, he wasn't going to stick around to find out what was wrong. He'd go knock on the rest room door and tell her to hurry. He could always plead that his ribs had taken a turn for the worse.

But it was the situation which was taking a turn for the worse. He knew it with growing certainty as he made his way down the paneled hall to the door discreetly marked "ladies." Even as he knocked, he was already afraid of not getting a response.

What the hell could be wrong?

But something *was* wrong. Terribly wrong. There was no one inside the rest room as Dev discovered when he impatiently disregarded the proprieties and pushed open the door. No one at all.

The gardens. Perhaps she'd decided to take a quick look at the gardens that had been described in the brochure. One could only see a portion of them from the dining room, and he knew she'd been intrigued by the idea of the maze somewhere in the middle.

Damn it, if she'd decided to take a quick trip outside without telling him…! He cut off the thought with a disgusted grimace. He'd hardly given her any reason to think she shouldn't go outside alone. How could he blame her if she'd dashed out for a quick peek at the maze? The perspiration was beginning to dampen his khaki shirt as he started down the hall toward the entrance to the formal gardens. He should have told her he was in great pain. He ought to have pleaded much more severe discomfort. Then she wouldn't have decided to take the little side trip to the gardens.

Outside on the wide veranda he stood gazing at the sweep of heavily landscaped grounds. Over a century of carefully assisted growth had created a near labyrinth of luscious plantings. Magnificent, tall hedges, huge shade trees and tangled thickets of exotic flowers all combined to form a dense pattern of foliage which stretched across a couple of acres. Some formal garden! The jungle appeared to have had a strong influence during the years. There was no way he could see anything clearly beyond the first few yards.

There was no sign of Tabitha. No sign of anyone, in fact. The gardens were silent.

Dev's fingers tightened on the cane as he considered his options. There weren't a whole lot of them. Maybe she'd gone in search of the maze. It was supposed to be somewhere in the middle of that conglomeration of greenery.

Before he'd made it past the first few ten-foot-high hedges, Dev knew disaster hovered near. The prickly feeling down his spine was rapidly turning into a full-scale alarm.

When he rounded the next wall of boxwood he was almost prepared for the sight that awaited him.

Tabitha was there all right. She was standing very still, her huge eyes wide and fearful as she gazed at him.

The man with the gun in his hand had his free palm clamped firmly over her mouth. He was thin, lanky and his long hair was dark and greasy looking.

"It's about time you came looking for her, Colter. Thought we might have to send a message or something. But Waverly was pretty sure you'd come looking when your girl friend didn't return to the dining room."

Steve Waverly, the irritating weasel who had tried to dance with Tabitha two nights before, sauntered out from behind a hedge. He still had that California beach-boy grin, Dev thought disgustedly.

"Game's over, Colter," he said laconically. "Let's have the film."

Only years of training kept Dev from gritting his teeth in self-disgust. How could he have been so stupid? He should have guessed that Waverly had been after more than just Tabitha. Who the hell was he and how did he know about the film?

Something about being around Tabitha had dulled his highly developed senses, Dev decided grimly. Around her, other things seemed more important. He could only hope that his lapse wasn't going to cost both of them their lives.

Six

"Let her go, Waverly. Tabby's not involved in this." Dev didn't really expect that bit of logic to have much of an effect and it didn't. Steve Waverly just smiled a little more broadly and shook his head.

"Now, you know I'm not about to do that. Not until I have the film. Then as far as I'm concerned both of you can go back to the ship. In the meantime Miss Graham here is going to play the part of incentive for you."

Tabitha's eyes flickered warily from one man to the other. The long-haired man with the gun who was holding her never said a word. It was clear Waverly was the one in charge. Dev concentrated on him, trying not to see the fear in Tabitha's questioning gaze.

"Waverly," he said very softly, "I told you the other night that if you came near her again I'd take you apart. And that was just if you asked her to dance.

Can you imagine what I'm going to do to you for manhandling her like this?''

The toothy smile sagged for a fraction of a second before it was tacked firmly back in place. Good, Dev decided sardonically, he hadn't completely lost the old charm. He could still put a trace of fear in a man like Steve Waverly, even though Waverly's henchman held a gun. Too bad he simply hadn't dumped the younger man over the side of the ship when he'd first made a nuisance of himself. Would have saved a lot of trouble.

"Your lady friend isn't going to get hurt and neither are you. All we're after is that film you picked up on St. Regis. Then the two of you can go back to being happy-go-lucky cruise passengers.'' Waverly threw a derisive glance at Tabitha, who was watching him as if he were a snake. "That is if your tabby cat—wasn't that what you called her?—if she doesn't mind continuing to play the role of convenient cover for you. Will you mind that, Miss Graham? Now that you know what's going on, are you going to object to sleeping with him? He just used you to give himself a little protective camouflage, you know. Paired off with you, he appeared to be merely another male passenger who was having a good time on board ship. Helped him pass the time very pleasantly, I imagine. Kept him from getting bored.''

Tabitha made a muffled sound behind the hard palm that was slapped across her mouth. The words were unintelligible but her eyes were blazing. It occurred to Dev that she was not only terrified; she was furious. If her temper was akin to her passion, Tabitha Graham might turn into one hell of a dangerous commodity when angered. Strangely enough, it would have been impossible before now to even imagine her truly furious. She was such a gentle little thing!

"She's not interested in your analysis of our relationship, Waverly. Let her go."

"Not a chance.'

"I haven't got the film," Dev said wearily. "It's back on board the ship. Hidden in my cabin."

"I don't believe you. You wouldn't let it out of your sight until you handed it over to your boss. We both know that!"

"Do we?" Dev inquired with deceptive mildness.

"Tell him to shut up and hand over the film, Steve," the long-haired man whispered urgently. He was clearly much more nervous than Waverly. Which didn't make for a good situation. If there was one thing worse than a man with a gun, it was a nervous man with a gun.

"Don't worry. Mr. Colter will cooperate, I'm sure. We just have to convince him we're quite serious." Waverly made a production out of lighting a cigarette as if he had all the time in the world. Given the fact that no one else seemed to be wandering down into the gardens from the hotel, that might be quite true, Dev was forced to acknowledge.

"How did you learn about the pickup on St. Regis?" he asked as if only idly curious.

"The man who tried to stop you in that alley survived." Waverly smiled, narrowing his eyes against the smoke from his cigarette. "I guess you didn't know about that interesting tidbit, did you? We found him in the trash bin at the far end of the alley where you'd stuffed him after you practically killed him. Did you think he was dead?''

"I wasn't sure," Dev said dryly. "I knew he was unconscious, though, and I didn't want to leave him lying around to litter the streets." Well, hell. It had taken almost the last of his strength to dump that guy into the trash bin in the hope that he wouldn't be discovered for some time. Looked like it had all been a wasted effort. Out of the corner of his eye Dev saw Tabitha looking at him incredulously. This whole thing must be coming as one hell of a shock to her. Later he would try to explain everything. Right now he had business to transact.

"Well, he made it, and he gave me the identification I needed on you. Our information was that whoever was assigned to the pickup would be traveling on board the cruise ship, but we couldn't be sure which passenger was our rabbit. Once Jeffers managed to tell me about the tall bastard with the cane, I was able to spot you." Waverly glanced at Tabitha, who glared back. "I'll admit I couldn't figure you out, Miss Graham. Definitely not Colter's type from what we knew of him. Then I finally realized he was just using you for cover. Sorry you had to get involved in all of this but that's the breaks, I guess." He stepped toward her. "Speaking of breaks…" Almost casually he fingered the line of her jaw. "I'd hate to have to resort to breaking various and sundry bones in your soft little body."

"Get away from her Waverly!" Dev snapped, ice layering every word. He watched, trying to keep his glance stony as Waverly turned toward him. Then the other man smiled bleakly and very slowly allowed his hand to trail down the line of Tabitha's throat to the curve of her breast. Dev knew he was on the edge of losing his control completely as he watched the other man touching Tabitha with such obscene intimacy. *"Get away from her!"*

"Sure, Colter. Just as soon as you hand over the film."

"You can have the goddamned film. Just turn her loose!' Dev growled savagely.

Waverly stepped forward a couple of feet and politely extended his hand. "Film first, I'm afraid."

Tabitha tensed, knowing she was never going to have another chance. The thin, lanky man with the greasy, long hair was concentrating almost completely on the drama the other two men were acting out. It had to be now or never.

With a muffled shout, she twisted, throwing herself sideways against the man with the gun. He really wasn't all that much heavier than herself, she realized distractedly.

He yelled as she fell against him, stumbling awkwardly beneath the unexpected assault.

"Tabby!"

She heard Dev call her name as she toppled to the ground on top of her victim but all she could think about was the gun. The thin young man was proving to be far stronger than he looked. She would never be able to outfight him. He squirmed violently beneath her, still gripping the gun, although he couldn't yet raise his arm to use it.

"You bitch!" he shouted tightly, lashing at her with his free hand. "Get off me, you damned bitch!"

Almost simultaneously Tabitha heard Dev's cane

whistle through the air in a violent arc that cracked against Waverly's face. Then, just as she realized how hopeless her own attack was going to prove, Dev was in front of her, his foot coming down on the gunman's arm. The man screamed, but his hand clenched spasmodically around the handle of the pistol instead of releasing it.

With a desperate heave the thin man threw off the scrabbling Tabitha, sending her crashing against Dev, who staggered briefly under the unexpected impact of her body. Instantly Tabitha pushed free, scrambling to her feet, but she didn't need to hear Dev's short, explicit oath to know that it was too late.

"Waverly! The gun!" The long-haired man on the grass hurled the weapon frantically at his companion even as the edge of Dev's hand came down against the side of his neck in a devastating blow that rendered him unconscious.

Dev stumbled awkwardly as he tried to regain his balance after delivering the karate chop. He cursed the cane and the stiff leg which was slowing him down. Time was running out. He would never be able to get to Waverly in time. The other man, holding his head with one hand where the cane had drawn blood, was just closing his fingers around the handle of the gun.

"Tabitha! The maze!" Dev steadied himself with the cane and jerked at Tabitha's wrist. Without pausing he yanked her after him as he plunged into the narrow entrance of the dense, boxwood maze. God! He would have given his soul in that moment for the old speed and coordination that he had once taken for granted along with the rest of his acute senses.

At least Tabby had the sense to keep her mouth shut and not demand explanations at this point, Dev thought with some satisfaction as he pulled her deeper and deeper into the maze. He relied on instinct to orient him.

Tabitha wasn't asking questions because she was too busy fighting down panic and anger. The walls of the maze loomed incredibly high, blocking out much of the sun; the dense foliage was so thick it was impossible to see from one aisle into the next. This was a real maze, she thought in stunned wonder, not just some gardener's whimsy. Whoever had constructed it originally had intended for the final product to be a real challenge. What did Dev think he was going to accomplish by dragging both of them in here?

Then again, he might have decided there wasn't much to lose. Waverly had the gun. She and Dev were unarmed.

Even as that realization dawned, Dev was halting her, pushing her flat against the prickly wall of the corridor in which they now stood. An instant later, Tabitha understood why he had stopped. The corridor was a dead end.

He turned to her, silver eyes like slivers of steel. Tabitha stared up at him in dumbfounded amazement. This wasn't the man she knew. This couldn't be the gentle, vulnerable, self-effacing man she had seduced last night! This Dev Colter was a man of forceful action and danger. She realized she was almost as afraid of him as she was of Steve Waverly and the thin man who had held the gun on her. Tabitha's mouth was abruptly dry.

"Don't move. Not an inch," he growled almost

soundlessly. "And don't say a word. We're only going to get one chance. Nod your head if you understand."

Mutely Tabitha inclined her head once in a jerky little nod. Her nails pressed anxiously into her palms. He continued to stare down at her a second longer, and then he turned back toward the entrance of the dead-end corridor in which they stood.

Tabitha stayed where she was, pressed flat against the boxwood wall, and stared after him. He moved soundlessly on the grass which carpeted the maze, but she had the feeling that he would have moved just as lightly over dried twigs or stones. Even with his obvious dependency on the cane, there was a feral quality about Dev, a quality she ought to have noticed long before this. Why hadn't she?

The answer came almost at once: Because she had wanted to see another kind of man altogether. Her imagination had created as unreal a beast as any that ever graced a medieval bestiary. Now she was faced with the very real man behind the fabulous construct created by her own desires.

She watched, aware that there was another beast prowling the maze besides Dev. Steve Waverly had followed them through the boxwood entrance, and there was no reason to think he had turned around and retreated. He would know his quarry was unarmed and he seemed to want something Dev had.

Dev halted for a moment before stepping out into the next angled aisle of the maze. Tabitha heard the faintest of soft, snicking noises as he lifted the cane for a moment, and then, to her fascinated horror, she saw the wicked, steel blade that had emerged from the tip of the cane. Her eyes were glued to the deadly sword as Dev glanced back over his shoulder. The intent mask of his features grew colder and more brutal than ever.

Slowly she raised her eyes to his face, and Dev wanted to curse aloud at the expression he saw in them. For God's sake! Did she think he could take care of Waverly by being Mr. Nice Guy? The sword cane was little enough defense against the gun as it was. She looked as if she didn't want him to have even that much of a weapon!

No, he told himself in the next breath, it wasn't that she wished him unarmed. She wished him to disappear, along with the entire situation. Hell, he was going to have his hands full trying to pacify her after this was all over. She was clearly half in shock. Abruptly he turned away, not wanting to suffer another instant of that accusing, pleading glance. First things first.

Soundlessly he slipped out into the adjoining passage. His stiff leg kept him from the smooth, gliding pace which had once been his to use at will, but at least it didn't keep him from being able to move altogether. He didn't dare rely on the cane now. It had to be kept ready for the instant it would be needed. How far into the maze had Waverly come?

Dev paused to listen, trying to revive all the old instincts and the once-highly attuned senses. Too bad he hadn't listened to those senses earlier. He might have been able to avoid this stupid mess altogether. If anything happened to Tabby, it would be all his fault. The thought made him clench the ebony cane more violently than ever. Deliberately he relaxed the grip. Tension wasn't going to do him any good. It obscured the awareness he needed at the moment.

There, behind him, back toward the entrance to the maze. He turned cautiously, willing the faint, rasping sound to repeat itself. Slowly he made his way down the narrow corridor. Would Waverly be fool enough to blunder through the maze looking for him? Or would he realize the danger of hunting when you couldn't see around the next corner? Dev glanced down at the tip of the sword in his hand. All he needed was an instant's warning. Just one lousy instant of advantage.

The rasping sound came again. Waverly was moving deeper into the maze, certain he held the only weapon. Dev felt the infuriating stiffness in his knee and gritted his teeth. He had told Delaney he had no business getting back into this life. A man pushing forty and cursed with a game leg was hardly prime material for this kind of work.

The faint, rasping sound came once more. Waverly was either not terribly worried about giving away his location, or he simply didn't know how to move silently. The younger man would be in a hurry to wind up the situation before other tourists came wandering down into the garden. Perhaps that urgency would make the damn beach boy careless. Dev deliberately slowed his breathing, striving to focus all his attention on his sense of hearing. Then the boxwood wall beside him vibrated ever so slightly.

Waverly was in the neighboring passage.

The question, Dev realized grimly, was how could he be certain which end of the passage would be open. He might turn the corner up ahead and find himself facing another wall of thick boxwood. Or he might find himself facing Waverly's gun.

The only sensible thing to do was to station himself at the intersection ahead and wait. Waiting was one thing he could do far better than Waverly could. Younger men tended to be far more impatient. Yeah, Dev told himself evenly, I'll wait this one out.

He advanced to the intersection and then pressed his back to the wall, his head turned to the side so that he could watch the opening. Eventually Waverly would find his way past this corridor entrance. The maze wasn't so complicated that it couldn't be searched by someone intent on doing exactly that. At least in this position, Dev thought, he was between Waverly and Tabitha. She was in a dead-end corridor and there weren't any other intersections between him and her except the one he had just come through.

And Waverly was still on the other side of the boxwood wall. Dev could hear the faint sound of the other man's breathing now. Then Waverly lost his patience altogether.

"Listen to me, Colter," he hissed, his voice so unexpectedly close that Dev instinctively tensed. "All I want is the film. Bring it to the front of the maze and I'll let both of you go."

Sure you will, Dev thought silently. What kind of a fool do you think I am, kid? Just keep coming this way.

"Can you hear me, Colter?"

Dev waited silently. Waverly's voice was a little farther away now. Was he going to search another corridor before he came down the one which formed the intersection Dev was guarding? Apparently so.

The waiting was always the worst part. But when your life depended on it, you learned to wait. Patiently.

The minutes clicked past. Occasionally Waverly called out persuasively, but Dev just went on waiting. Sooner or later the man had to come down this corridor.

Steve Waverly eventually made his way down the narrow passage which joined with the one in which Dev stood. The younger man was making very little effort to cover the sound of his movements now. It was obvious he was getting nervous about the unfinished business. It was that nervousness which gave Dev his opportunity.

Waverly came down the corridor at a trot, moving much too hastily and too noisily. Dev gathered himself. As he had told Tabby, there was only going to be one chance. He waited one more excruciating second, buying all the advantage he could.

Then, when he sensed that Waverly was only a couple of feet from the intersection, Dev threw himself out into the passage, the blade of the sword cane slashing unerringly around in a curve, searching for its prey.

Steve Waverly yelled in astonishment as his intended victim emerged from the corridor to the right, but before he could squeeze off a shot, cold steel had sliced a scarlet ribbon across the arm which held the weapon. The gun fell from nerveless fingers. Waverly screamed again and clutched at his bleeding arm.

"Don't move or the next thing I slash will be your throat."

Dev emphasized his words by letting the tip of the

sword cane lie menacingly alongside Waverly's neck. The blond man froze, his eyes glazed with pain and fear. Cautiously, the sword never moving an inch, Dev balanced himself on his good leg and used the other to kick the gun farther out of reach. He didn't dare attempt to lean down and pick it up. The awkward movement might make his balance too precarious. Damned leg.

"All right, Waverly. Let's go. Turn around and head back toward the entrance."

"For God's sake! I'm bleeding to death!"

"You'll live. Unfortunately. Now *move!*"

"Listen, Colter. We can make a deal here. I'll split the profit off that damn film. You can have Eddie's share."

"Eddie's your good buddy lying unconscious out there on the grass?"

"That's right. Forget him. You can have his portion."

"Why do I get this nasty feeling that you can't be relied on, Waverly?" Dev prodded his victim gently with the cane, and the man moved uneasily back down the corridor.

"You can trust me."

"Sure. Even if I could, I'd still want to slit your throat for the way you used my woman. That was a mistake, Waverly. A bad one. Give me half an excuse right now, and I'll kill you for that."

"I didn't hurt her!"

"You threatened her. And you touched her. Didn't I tell you just the other night that I'd take you apart if you came near her?"

"Colter, listen to me!"

"Oh, shut up, Waverly. Just keep moving."

"Which way? I'm lost." Waverly glared furiously around as he came to a halt at the next intersection.

"To the right," Dev said automatically, his sense of direction as sound as it had ever been in the past. Some instincts, apparently, didn't fade. "Now left."

Without hesitation Dev followed the proddings of his inner senses, pushing Waverly through the entrance of the maze a couple of minutes later. "Lie down on the grass over there by your good friend Eddie." He waited as Waverly did as he was told.

"What about my arm?"

"What about it?" Dev asked carelessly. Then he raised his voice. "Tabby! Can you hear me? Come on out of the maze."

There was a moment's silence.

"Tabby!"

"I hear you, Dev." Her voice sounded very faint.

"Come on out. Everything's under control." Hell, his tone still sounded gruff, Dev realized vaguely. It was hard to leach out the violence when your body still hummed with it. "Tabby!" he tried again.

"Dev, I'm trying but it's confusing."

"What the hell...?"

"It's a maze, Dev, remember?" There was a touch of asperity in the question. Her voice sounded even more faint.

"Tabby, I can't come and get you. I've got to keep an eye on Waverly. Listen, on your way out, watch for the gun he dropped. Bring it with you."

There was no answer this time. Dev waited again, but now he didn't feel patient. He wanted to see her again, reassure himself that she was safe, and then he

wanted to get rid of Waverly and friend. The sooner
this mess was cleaned up, the better. Delaney could
handle what was left of it. Dev knew that all he himself wanted was to return to the ship with Tabby. He
was going to be busy enough explaining everything
to her.

Three more minutes ticked past.

"Tabby? What's keeping you? Just walk back out
the same way we went in."

"I'm not sure which way that is! And stop yelling
at me!"

"I'm not yelling at you. But I haven't got all day!"

"Then just go ahead and leave without me!" she
called back furiously.

At the caustic tone in her words Dev winced. She
was more than a little upset, he realized. "Tabby?"

"I think I'm at the center of the maze."

"Orient yourself with the sun!" he called back,
aware that he must sound rather irritated by now.
"Hurry up."

This time he received no answer at all. Several
more minutes went by. Dev felt his annoyance growing. Was she playing games with him? If that was the
case... "About time you got here!" he muttered as
she suddenly appeared at the entrance. He had never
been so happy to see anyone in his life.

But his expression didn't convey his relief. Tabitha
emerged to find him glaring at her, and she froze for
an instant at the tableau of the three men. Dev was
standing guard with the edge of the sword hovering
close to a sullen-looking Waverly. The thin young
man on the ground hadn't yet awakened. Tabitha
swallowed and wondered if he might be dead.

"I see you found the gun. Good. Bring it here,
Tabby." There was a sense of exaggerated patience
in his tone which thoroughly annoyed Tabitha. This
was all his fault in the first place! Wordlessly she
went forward and handed over the gun. As soon as
he had it in his hand, Dev sheathed the sword in the
cane with a small movement of his finger on a hidden
button. Then he leaned against the ebony stick with
a stifled groan.

Tabitha resolutely ignored the sign of pain. Never
again was he going to deceive her with his small,
insidious tricks! Her chin came up and her eyes narrowed. "Now what?" she asked aloofly.

He slanted her an assessing glance. "Now we get
rid of these two. I suppose you'd better go back to
the hotel and get some help. Have them call the local
police. I'll have to explain all this to the authorities."

Obediently Tabitha swung around, grateful for any
excuse to depart the violent scene.

"Tabby?"

She glanced back warily. "What?"

"If you couldn't remember which way we had
gone into the maze, how did you find your way out
from the center so quickly?"

She shrugged. "I remembered something I read
somewhere about how to escape from mazes."

He stared at her in surprise. "What's that?"

"You put your hand against the wall and never lift
it off. That way you don't go over the same territory
twice." She couldn't keep a tinge of pride out of her
voice even though she was still furious and resentful.

"Tabby, that's just an old myth! If that's the tech-

nique you used then you were merely very lucky!''
Dev growled.

"An old myth? But, Dev, I'm something of an
expert on old myths, remember? And on the whole
I've found them to be much more reliable than modern lies told by modern men like you." Without waiting for a response, Tabitha turned back toward the
hotel.

Damn! Dev thought, it's going to be a long night.
He glared down at Waverly. "You're to blame for all
this, you stupid bastard. Why the hell did you have
to get so damn greedy?"

Waverly, wisely sensing that his luck had already
run out, kept his mouth shut.

The island police, spiffy in their summer-weight,
khaki uniforms, arrived twenty minutes later. Tabitha
did not return with them.

By the time Dev had explained the situation, put
through a call to Delaney from police headquarters
and managed to extricate himself from the sticky
scene, he was not in a good mood. Delaney had taken
the whole thing much too cavalierly as far as Dev
was concerned.

"You've still got the magic touch, Dev," Delaney
announced cheerily from the other end of the line. "I
told you that you did."

"The old touch, my ass. I nearly got killed, Delaney. What's more I nearly got my woman killed. I
was a fool to let you talk me into this. Oh, hell, why
am I standing here in this nearly one-hundred-percent
humidity trying to reason with you? You've got a
one-track mind."

"That's how I got where I am. Plus instincts, of

course. I've got good instincts, too, Dev. Just like you. We're two of a kind."

Dev closed his eyes in disgust. His leg was aching again. He wondered what the odds were of getting Tabitha to massage it for him. "Listen, Delaney, we can argue this out later. The ship sails in forty minutes, and I'm going to be on it. I'll make the delivery when I return to the States. In the meantime, try to keep creeps like Waverly out of my way, will you? This was supposed to be a trouble-free assignment designed to help me get my feet wet again as I recall."

Delaney laughed. "See you soon, Dev. Enjoy the rest of your cruise." He hung up the phone before Dev could think of a suitably cutting response. So much for Washington, D.C. types. Bastards. Now it was time to go back to the ship and deal with Washington, state of, types. Sweet, little tabby cats who had had their fur ruffled the wrong way.

He would soon stroke Tabby back into a warm and purring mood, Dev promised himself as he took his leave of the somewhat confused island police. "Don't worry, someone will be along soon to pick up Waverly and good, old Eddie there," he assured the chief. "Just keep them under lock and key until then, okay?"

"Of course, Mr. Colter, we are only too anxious to cooperate. But we would like a few explanations," the balding, middle-aged man informed him with a frown. He was a good cop and he didn't like confusing situations caused by visiting Americans. Americans were always confusing, it was true, but this instance was a bit more annoying than usual.

STEPHANIE JAMES   139

"The gentleman who arrives to take charge of these two will be happy to explain everything," Dev said smoothly. Damned if he was going to hang around and make excuses. The first priority was to get back to the ship and find Tabitha.

She was probably hiding in her cabin even now, nervous and anxious and full of questions. He'd rather answer her queries than those of the chief of police, Dev decided, flagging down a taxi.

Poor Tabby. She had been through a lot this afternoon. Actually, he owed her a favor. If she hadn't made that move against the guy with the gun, things might have been far more complicated than they had been. Dev smiled to himself as the cab whisked him back to the docks where the tender boats were making their last runs to the ship. She had plenty of spirit, and she'd kept her head when the chips were down. He realized he couldn't wait until he had her back in his arms.

He would explain everything, and then he would make sweet love to her until she had forgiven him for the upsetting afternoon. There wasn't a doubt in his mind that she *would* forgive him. How could someone as compassionate and gentle as Tabby Graham refuse to accept his apologies? It was only a matter of time before he once more had her in the palm of his hand. Dev relaxed a little at the thought.

But sweet, compassionate, gentle Tabitha Graham was not in her cabin. She was, in fact, nowhere on board the luxury liner. And the huge ship had sailed before Dev, grilling everyone from the lowliest steward to the captain, discovered that Tabby had returned to the liner only long enough to collect her things from the stateroom.

Then she had left once more, heading for the island airport, where she had caught the first plane back to the mainland.

Trapped on board until the ship reached its next destination, Dev spent the evening alone in his cabin with a bottle of whiskey. After every swallow he glared at the ebony cane which concealed the bit of microfilm in a hidden compartment in the handle.

It had been a damned Washington, D.C. type who had designed that cane.

Turkeys.

Dev took another swallow of whiskey and made up his mind. He was going to get as far away from Washington, D.C. as soon as possible.

Seven

A week after her return to Port Townsend a rare fury still smoldered in Tabitha's heart.

Devlin Colter had used her.

Every time the thought of being used crossed her mind, Tabitha experienced another blazing surge of anger. Never had she known any emotion as fierce and violent as the rage she had felt since that fateful afternoon in the maze.

No, that wasn't strictly accurate, she was honest enough to admit a few days after her return. There had once been another kind of emotion that had flared just as wildly and had been just as rare. She had learned of the other fire the night she had seduced Dev.

Passion and anger. She had never known the meaning of either as she did in the wake of her experience with Dev Colter. Seven days after her escape from the island, Tabitha concentrated fiercely on the anger. The memory of her own passion was far more disturbing and better left alone as much as possible. She threw herself back into work at her shop, The Manticore.

Dev had toyed with her, played a game of pretend. Tabitha gritted her teeth every time the realization went through her mind. She would be unpacking a carton of books and find her fingers trembling with fury as she tried to wield the knife she was using on the cardboard.

Or she would be thumbing through her beautiful collection of bestiaries and come across a picture of a dragon. The sight of it would cause her to snap the book shut with a brutal movement.

A game of make-believe. Why had he indulged such a silly pastime? Just because he thought she made a good cover for his activities? Because he had been bored? Because she had been the one to get him out of that alley and he had felt a fleeting gratitude?

None of the possibilities was pleasant, and none of them did anything to soothe her fury.

God, what a fool she had made of herself! How he must have laughed to himself that night when she had set out to seduce him by plying him with drinks and tales of the mating habits of the animals in her medieval books! The red stained her cheeks once more as she remembered that awful night.

Ten days after her return home, Tabitha was shelving new paperback mysteries in her shop when the memory of her own passion danced, unbidden, once more through her mind. This time her hand stilled in the act of placing a book in the rack.

This time her fingers didn't shake with fury and humiliation.

For a long moment Tabitha simply stared unseeingly at the book in her hand, her face revealing the absorption of her own thoughts. Damn it, she had known passion, real passion that night. She had thought herself in love, and she had set out to seduce the man of her dreams.

Whatever else you could say about that embarrassing and infuriating evening, she had been successful. She had made love to her dragon and even if he had been secretly laughing at her, he had responded.

There could be no doubt about that! she reminded herself feelingly. And he hadn't been the only one who had responded. Her own reaction had been deeply, startlingly fulfilling; unlike anything else she had ever known.

It was true that she had been making love to a myth—a man who didn't really exist except in her own imagination—but she had done it rather well. Yes, damn it, she *had* done it rather well. Dev Colter might have been amusing himself with her, or he might have been deliberately using her, but he had been satisfied that night, she would stake The Manticore on that small fact.

Tabitha's gentle mouth twisted wryly as she shelved the last of the mysteries and headed back toward the front counter. If only he had been the man he had pretended to be: a wonderfully vulnerable, sensitive, shy man who had needed her. How perfect it all would have been.

The chiming of the bell on the door broke into her morbid reverie. With an effort of will Tabitha forced herself to remember that she had a business to run and that meant summoning up a pleasant welcome for potential customers. The young couple who entered looked like the professional, browsing type but one never knew.

"We saw the poster of the phoenix in the window and wondered if you have a copy for sale?" the man inquired politely. His girl friend, her long hair in braids, looked hopeful.

"It's a beautiful poster," she said quickly.

"I've got several in stock," Tabitha informed them, striving for a gracious tone as she delved under the counter to find the rolled up, plastic-encased posters. "Take your pick. Phoenixes are popular with artists."

The young couple pored over the various paintings and sketches of the mythological bird, most of which depicted the creature in the classic pose of rising from its own ashes.

"I think this one would look good on the living room wall," the young woman finally announced decisively. "It's got all the right colors for that room."

Idly Tabitha glanced at the poster that had been selected. "You picked one of the more accurate paintings," she approved. "A lot of analysts think the phoenix was probably a purple heron which got sacrificed to an Egyptian sun god periodically. The bird in that painting looks nice and purple."

"Our interior designer would call it mauve," the young man said, grinning good-naturedly. "Okay, we'll take this one. When we get it framed, it's going to be fabulous."

Tabitha nodded, dutifully writing up the transaction

and handing over a rolled copy of the elegant poster. As the couple turned to leave the shop she began re-rolling the rest of the phoenix collection. There was quite a variety in the artwork, some of which had been commissioned by Tabitha herself specifically for sale in the shop, but all of the art showed a regal bird gloriously reborn after a fiery death. The pictures struck a responsive chord in her own mind.

She, herself, had gone up in flames that night she had seduced Dev Colter. What were the odds that, like the phoenix, she, too could be reborn?

The tantalizing thought came and went in her head all during the long afternoon. Whenever the shop door opened, it interrupted some variation on the teasing possibility of becoming a different woman. Damn it, she *had* been a different woman that night she had lain in Dev Colter's arms. She had been vibrant and alive and passionate.

Why couldn't she be that way again? Deliberately Tabitha went to the special section of the shop where she housed the reproductions of medieval bestiaries and took down several of the magnificently illustrated volumes. Hauling them over to the counter, she opened each one to the section on the phoenix and began to read.

Phoenixes, it seemed, only went through their fiery regeneration once every five hundred years. Well, allowances would have to be made on that score, Tabitha told herself dryly. She was going to turn thirty in another couple of days; surely that milestone in a woman's life could substitute for the five-hundred-year mark of a phoenix's! She stared at all the various woodcuts and drawings of the birds, moodily trying to imagine herself as a renewed and entirely different woman. A woman like she had been that night on the ship.

But such a woman needed a man to appreciate the radical change, Tabitha told herself derisively. Where was she going to find such a male? She knew plenty of people, having lived in town for the past six years, but they all saw her as she was, a quiet, unassuming woman who hadn't been able to hold onto a husband for more than a few months. They had all felt very sorry for her when Greg had left, of course, but Tabitha doubted that any of them had been very surprised.

What she needed was a way of formally announcing her new image, Tabitha decided. She would give herself a thirtieth birthday party.

It was a cinch no one else would remember to give her one!

With the care and precision of a determined military commander, Tabitha devoted herself to the plans for her thirtieth birthday party. Just the act of organizing it was something of a catharsis. Her pent-up rage and humiliation gave her the necessary energy to see the huge undertaking through. She had never planned anything on such a scale in her life, and it took more work than she would have imagined.

"You want two cases of that Cabernet?" her friend at the wine shop asked dubiously. "Are you sure you don't mean just two bottles?" He knew as well as anyone else in the neighborhood that Tabitha Graham did not entertain on a grand scale.

"Two cases, George," Tabitha confirmed, "and a case of the Sauvignon Blanc '81, too. Now let me see your cheese selection. And I'll want a large quantity of sourdough bread, too. Can you order that for me?''

''Well, sure, but, if you don't mind my asking, why do you need so much food and wine, Tabitha?'' George Royce scratched his graying head and smiled at her with curiosity.

''For my thirtieth birthday party, George. Oh, by the way, you and your wife are invited. Bring anybody else you can think of, too, please.''

''Anybody else? How big a party is this going to be?''

''As big as I can make it!''

The sign went up in the bookshop window the day before the event. Done by a friend who had an art gallery down the street from Tabitha's bookshop, it depicted a beautiful version of a phoenix and announced to all and sundry that everyone was invited to Tabitha's home the following day.

''You're going to get some freeloaders with an open invitation like that,'' Sandra Adams warned as she walked into the shop that afternoon.

''That's all right. I've got plenty of food. A few freeloaders won't matter,'' Tabitha declared airily. ''Are you coming, Sandy?''

''Oh, sure. Wouldn't miss it. Everyone's coming. We're all a little curious. What happened to you on that cruise, Tab? You seem different, somehow.''

Tabitha smiled serenely. She had taken to wearing all her clothes without a bra this past week, and more than one person had commented on the ''change'' in her. And she'd caught more than one pair of male eyes straying to the loose fitting shirts she was wearing with her jeans. The open attention was still a little awkward to handle at times, but Tabitha was grimly sticking to the plan.

"I had a wonderful time. Found out what I've been missing all these years, Sandy. You wouldn't believe how people act on those cruise ships."

"I've heard stories." Sandy grinned. "To tell you the truth, Tab, I think it's terrific. I mean, the change is for the better. You seem more lively somehow. Even Ron noticed it."

"Is he coming?" Ron was Sandy's brother, who visited frequently from Seattle.

"You bet. He was planning on coming to Port Townsend this weekend anyway with a couple of friends. They'll be there. You know Ron. Offer him free beer and food and he'll turn up for anything."

Several young tourists in the shop jokingly called attention to the sign and asked if it truly was an open invitation. Tabitha assured them it was. To her delight a few said they might stop by on the evening of the party.

Tabitha used one of the books from the home entertaining section of The Manticore to help design the arrangement of food and beverages. Anxiously she went over and over the details, leaving nothing to chance. It was a bit frightening to plan a party of this magnitude. What if no one showed up?

That secret fear of all neophyte party-givers was still haunting her the evening of the party as she dressed in a dashing, black dress bought especially for the occasion from a friend who owned a boutique. The dress was a floating thing of sheer, black cotton designed with a wide, bateau neckline and full, dolman sleeves. It was bound at the waist with a wide, red leather belt that emphasized the curves above and below.

Any threat of poor attendance was dispelled almost as soon as Tabitha finished brushing her hair. The doorbell began to ring, and it didn't stop for the next hour and a half. Nearly everyone who had been invited and several others who had seen the sign in the shop window showed up to celebrate Tabitha's thirtieth birthday and to satisfy their curiosity about the change in Tabby Graham.

Circulating through her overcrowded living room, Tabitha did her best not to disappoint any of the curious. The blazing fire on the hearth made a fine focus for the event. Someone had already settled on the sheepskin rug in front of it.

"I never realized what a nice job you had done on this old cottage," Sandra Adams exclaimed, glancing around the room as Tabitha pushed a glass of wine into her hand. "I really love all those framed prints of your weird medieval animals. Somehow it all mixes very nicely with the black sofas and the polished wooden floors. And that rug under the glass coffee table is fantastic! Where did you get it?"

"It was a lucky find in Seattle." Tabitha smiled, glancing with just a trace of unease at the fringed rug she had once loved so much. It showed a fabulous dragon, complete with wings and gleaming eyes, and it reminded her far too vividly of the beaten and bloody dragon she had discovered in the alley on St. Regis. Both were creatures of myth, having no basis in reality.

"Oh, here's Ron and his friend now," Sandra observed, swinging toward the door as it opened to ad-

mit her handsome younger brother. Ron Adams was
about twenty-five and blessed with over six feet of
height. He worked out regularly at a Seattle health
club, and it showed in the well-sculpted lines of his
chest and shoulders. He wore his jet black hair in a
casual, windblown style that nicely complemented his
dark eyes and the tan he got skiing every winter.

The man who accompanied him was about the
same age and sported a dashing mustache. Both took
one look around at the lively throng and seemed to
approve.

"Over here, Ron!" Sandra called above the din.

Tabitha glanced assessingly at the younger man as
he approached. She had met Ron once or twice in the
past, but she doubted if it had been a memorable occasion for Sandra's good-looking brother.

"Hi, Tab, nice to see you again. Thanks for the
invitation," he drawled, his dark eyes running ap-
praisingly over the thin black cotton dress his hostess
was wearing.

Tabitha was learning to recognize that speculative
gleam in a man's eyes now. She had seen it more
than once this past week. The first time she'd ever
seen it had been when Dev Colter arrived at her door
the morning she had chosen not to wear a bra for the
first time. That particular undergarment was tucked
away in her lingerie drawer tonight, too. Gamely she
ignored a twinge of self-consciousness and summoned up her brightest smile.

"I'm glad you could make it, Ron. And I hope your
friend enjoys himself."

"Oh, he will. Any beer?"

"Lots of it. Help yourself."

"Great. I'll be right back." His gaze strayed again to the black dress.

"Hmm," Sandra murmured as her brother disappeared in the direction of the serving area. "Why do I get this funny feeling that Ron is suddenly developing an interest in older women?"

Tabitha chuckled. "Not likely," she demurred. "But from my point of view, I have to admit I've heard some good things on the subject of younger men."

"Something along the line of 'Get 'em young and train 'em right'?" Sandra giggled. "Not a bad idea. Good luck with him, Tab."

Tabitha was aware of the embarrassed flush in her cheeks, but she managed a small grin.

Ron wasn't the only male who reassessed Tabitha Graham that night. As she determinedly threw herself into the role of hostess, Tabitha was aware of several glances, and there never seemed to be a lack of masculine assistance when she needed help opening new bottles of wine or carrying trays of appetizers.

On the one hand it was all very flattering, but on the other it didn't seem quite real. Or perhaps it was the free flow of wine which gave a tinge of unreality to the evening. The stereo was never silent, and the crowd in the living room seemed to swell rather than diminish throughout the evening. Thank heaven she had bought all those plastic glasses, Tabitha thought fleetingly at one point. She would long since have run out of her own glassware.

By one o'clock in the morning Tabitha was beginning to wonder how such an evening concluded itself. As far as she could tell no one seemed anxious to go home. Ron Adams was constantly around now, consuming her beer and wine in great quantities. His friend had disappeared long since with an attractive blonde whom Tabitha didn't recognize. Sandra Adams was involved in an intimate discussion with a young fisherman she had discovered near the fireplace. Throughout the room the laughter and the alcohol mingled.

By two o'clock some of the throng finally decided to take their leave. Tabitha, who had lost count of the glasses of wine she had consumed, cheerfully waved goodbye from her front porch and then turned back to the doorway to find Ron waiting with yet another glass for her.

"Great party, Tab," he mumbled quite thickly. His dark eyes gleamed once again with male speculation. "How old did you say you were?"

"Thirty," she murmured, sipping at her wine. Everything was beginning to take on a hazy, dreamy aspect that was really rather pleasant, she thought.

"I'm twenty-five," he told her and then smiled hugely. "I hear it's the latest trend."

Tabitha blinked, momentarily losing track of the conversation. It had been harder and harder to concentrate on such things for the past two hours. "Trend?"

"You know, men having affairs with women who are older."

"Ah, yes. The latest trend." Tabitha nodded wisely.

"There's something kind of exciting about it," Ron confided.

"I'm all for excitement."

"Me, too. Life is too damn short. Best thing you can do is fill it full of excitement," Ron agreed with a profundity born of a rather high percentage of alcohol in his bloodstream.

"Absolutely." Tabitha took another swallow of wine and somehow lost her balance on the porch. Carefully she put out a hand and braced herself against the wall. Then she smiled once more. "Get 'em young and train 'em right."

"Get what young?" Ron took a step closer and had to grab at the wall himself.

"Males."

"Male what?"

"Male whatever," Tabitha explained with a vague wave of her hand. "Puppies, dragons, basilisks, you name it. Best to get 'em young and train them properly. Older ones are likely to be mean and vicious."

"No kidding?"

"Yup."

"I want you to know," Ron said very carefully, if rather unsteadily, "that I consider myself very trainable." He edged a little close, using the wall for support.

"Good." Tabitha took another sip of wine and frowned intently. "First lesson is never bite the hand that feeds you."

"W-wouldn't dream of it," Ron assured her.

"Second lesson…" Tabitha paused, trying to concentrate. Then she brightened. "Is never to play games."

"No games." Ron draped his arm around her shoulders and raised his glass in salute to the second lesson.

"No playing make-believe," Tabitha emphasized just in case he hadn't got the message. "I have discovered that men who are older and more set in their ways have a nasty habit of playing make-believe. My first husband did, you know."

"The bastard!" Ron exclaimed with great feeling.

"He pretended he was in love with me," Tabitha explained gravely. "But he wasn't."

Ron shook his head, baffled at such duplicity.

"The last man I met also played make-believe. All kinds of games. He wasn't at all the sort of man he pretended to be."

"A rat."

"No, a dragon," she corrected automatically.

"Dragons are worse than rats."

"Yes."

Tabitha was about to go on with the lessons when the door behind them opened to reveal Sandra on the arm of the fisherman. "Oh, there you are, Tab. Jim and I were just leaving. Had a fantastic time. Happy birthday!"

"Thank you," Tabitha responded very politely.

"Think you can get home all right, Ron?" Sandra peered at her younger brother before the fisherman got her down the steps.

"Don't worry. I won't be driving. I'll walk," Ron said happily. "Then again maybe I won't go home at all."

"I see." Sandra tipped her head to one side and smiled at Tabitha. "You, uh, want me to see he gets home?"

"Heavens no! We're having a wonderful time,"

Tabitha assured her happily. "I'm giving him lessons."

Sandra slid a doubtful glance from Tabitha to her brother. "Interesting." Before she could say anything else the man named Jim tugged on her arm.

"Let's go, honey. It's late."

Sandra smiled. "Okay. Well, good night, you two. Be careful."

"Of what?" Tabitha asked very curiously.

"Never mind," Sandra groaned and let herself be hauled away by her new escort.

"Where were we?" Tabitha asked interestedly as Sandra and Jim climbed into a truck parked at the curb.

Ron's brows drew together in a thick line of forced effort. "Not sure. Next lesson was going to be number three, I think."

"Oh. Well, let's see. Ron, did I ever tell you about the mating habits of bestiary animals?" Tabitha began industriously. She'd had good luck with that technique once before, hadn't she?

"Nope." Ron swallowed the last of his wine. "How do they do it?"

"All sorts of fascinating ways," she told him gravely.

Once again the door to the house opened, however, interrupting Tabitha's words. This time a number of people were taking their departure, albeit reluctantly. By the time she got back to the conversation with Ron Adams the younger man had helped himself to still another glass of wine. He appeared to be having a great deal of difficulty in focusing. She managed to get him seated on one of the black couches before he toppled over, however.

After that accomplishment, Tabitha had to take another break to send off the last of her guests. Many of them had walked, and now they ambled happily back down the street towards their assorted homes. A few sang en route and there was a great deal of riotous laughter. Tabitha stood in her doorway and watched them go with a distinct sense of satisfaction.

It had been a very successful thirtieth birthday party. No doubt about it. And now it was time to get back to the business of seduction. There was a nice young man sitting on her couch just waiting for the techniques of an older, sophisticated woman. Tabitha smiled smugly as she turned back into the room.

"Animals!" Ron cried, hoisting his glass. "Tell me about the animals!" He leaned back into the corner, his feet propped on the cushions. Then he leered at Tabitha. "Always like to learn new things about animals. Almost became a zoologist instead of a sales rep, you know."

Tabitha blinked, studying her quarry craftily. Then she advanced farther into the room and sat down on the black couch across from him. Through the clear glass of the coffee table she could see the head of the dragon in the carpet.

"Such lovely silver eyes," she sighed, feeling a sudden wave of moroseness.

"Whose eyes?" Ron demanded aggressively.

"The dragon's."

"Umm. So how do dragons make love?" he asked with groggy interest.

Tabitha considered the question darkly, frowning down at the creature in the carpet.

"Magnificently. Once they're properly seduced, that is," she heard herself whisper in a blurry voice. Why did the dragon in the carpet have to stare up at her like that? He had no right to look so accusing. *He* was the one who should feel guilty! "But you can't trust them."

"Never trust dragons," Ron repeated dutifully. "Lesson number three." He waited expectantly.

"He has no right to make me feel guilty about this!" Tabitha hissed down at the carpet. "No right to interfere!"

"No right!" Ron agreed helpfully. Then he paused. "Who is 'he'?"

"The dragon."

"Damn right. No dragon's going to interfere."

"Nasty, vicious creature," Tabitha muttered, still staring down at the carpet.

"Probably an older dragon," Ron opined seriously.

"Nearly forty," Tabitha agreed with a nod.

"Much too old to be properly trained."

"You can't teach an old dragon new tricks," Tabitha sighed again. "They're born sneaky, though, so you probably couldn't teach a young one much, either."

"How about me?" Ron pressed with an inviting, if bleary, smile.

She glanced up, half-surprised to see him still there. She had been concentrating so hard on the damn dragon in the carpet that Ron had faded into insignificance. For a long moment she just looked at her last guest, trying to remember that she had planned

to seduce him. Then Tabitha closed her eyes with a
forlorn little groan. "It's no use, Ron. I can't go
through with it. You'd better leave now."

"Leave?" He sounded vastly dismayed.

Tabitha opened her eyes, aware of a very sleepy
sensation. "I can't seduce you tonight. I'm very sorry,
Ron. I just don't feel like talking about the beasts
anymore this evening."

"Not even a little bit?" he begged sorrowfully.

She shook her head. "I can't do it. Not with this
stupid dragon staring up at me."

"Maybe we could get rid of the dragon," Ron suggested helpfully.

"Wouldn't work. He'd still be around somewhere.
Oh, hell. I wonder how long he's going to hang
around like this, ruining my new life. Nasty, vicious
creature."

"It's not just your life he's ruining," Ron exploded
ruefully. "I think he's going to ruin my evening,
too."

Together with Tabitha he sat staring down at the
silent laughing dragon and then, very slowly, Ron
keeled over and fell asleep on the sofa he had been
occupying.

Tabitha glanced up and then leaned back into the
corner of her sofa and curled her feet under her. She
was so sleepy. Since the dumb dragon in the carpet
wasn't going to let her do anything else tonight, she
might as well get some rest. In the morning she would
figure out how she was going to get rid of the haunting presence in her home. Something had to be done.
She was making such terrific progress on other fronts,

she refused to let the dragon stand in her way when it came to organizing a whole new love life!

But even as she slid quickly off to sleep, Tabitha had the depressing feeling that it was going to be very difficult denying the dragon's claim. And her dreams were filled with images of a man with silver eyes and an ebony cane who kept fading in and out of the body of a dragon.

It was a long while before Tabitha separated the pounding in her head from the sound of pounding on her door. For long moments she lay very still, violently aware that daylight was streaming in through the curtains and that someone was at her front door.

Neither event was a welcome one.

"Oh, my God!" She shuddered, her hand going to her aching head. "Go away." But her voice was only a whisper, and it never carried as far as the door.

The knocking came more aggressively than ever.

"Oh, hell." Tabitha made a valiant effort and succeeded in rolling to the edge of the couch. Just as she did so a loud masculine snore came from the opposite sofa. Tabitha got her eyes open with an effort. The sight of Ron Adams sleeping across from her was a little too thought-provoking for eight o'clock in the morning. Even as she watched, he snored again and twisted a bit on the cushions.

Slowly Tabitha sat up, her hand still on her aching head. Memory returned in a cold rush as her eyes swept the littered room. Everything was in chaos. Empty glasses were stacked on all the tables and scattered on the floor. Overflowing ashtrays reeked with a stale, morning-after aroma. A chair had been overturned at some point and still lay on its side. The flowers were wilting in their bowls. Someone had spilled the water, apparently. It lay in a pool on the hardwood floor.

She hadn't thought to put any of the leftover food away, Tabitha realized as she got shakily to her feet. Partially consumed appetizers lay on paper plates scattered around the room. Half-drunk bottles of wine were still sitting on the serving table. The once cozy living room was a mess.

And then there was the man sleeping on her sofa.

Tabitha winced as she walked past Ron Adams' recumbent form. She might not be on cordial terms with dragons these days but she did owe the one on the floor a favor. He had kept her from making an idiot of herself with Ron Adams. At least her memory on that score was perfectly clear. Ron had passed out just before she had! The discussion on the mating habits of bestiary animals had not progressed as far as it had the last time she had brought up the subject with a man.

The knocking on the front door came once again.

"Okay, okay, I'm coming." It was a weak response and probably went unheard. Tabitha couldn't help it. She had to concentrate all her strength just to get across the room; there wasn't much energy left for shouting.

Desperately she attempted to plan a course of action as she crossed the room. The first thing was to get rid of whoever was pounding on her door. Then she would have to wake Ron Adams and get him out of the house.

Then she would have a nice, long shower, followed

by a huge cup of coffee. Following that, she would start cleaning house. Lord, what a day it was going to be.

"Will you kindly stop that damn pounding!" Tabitha commanded resentfully as she wrenched open the front door. "I'm opening the door as fast as I can!" Then her eyes went painfully wide as they took in the presence of the man on her doorstep. "Oh, my God," she breathed, stunned. "The dragon."

Dev Colter lowered the handle of the ebony cane, which he had been using to pound on the door. Bracing himself with it, he stared down at the rumpled, disheveled, bleary-eyed figure in front of him. The familiar silver eyes narrowed in mingled astonishment and gathering disapproval.

"What the hell happened to you?" he bit out.

Tabitha realized she was staring. Frantically she attempted to collect her scattered wits. "Dev," she managed weakly. "What are you doing here?"

"Isn't it rather obvious? I came to see you. Tabby, what on earth is going on here? You look awful." He scowled down at her, searching her face and the wrinkled black dress.

"Got run over by a herd of basilisks, I think," she got out in a thin voice. Maybe she was still dreaming. Perhaps she was still safely asleep on the couch and this was all some sort of crazy nightmare. Very cautiously she extended one hand and touched the unyielding surface of the blue, oxford cloth shirt he was wearing. "You're real, aren't you?" she groaned.

His scowl deepened and then he apparently decided he was getting nowhere trying to conduct a rational conversation on the doorstep. Stepping forward, he edged Tabitha aside and crossed the threshold into the chaotic room.

"Damn it to hell, Tabby. What went on here last night?" he snarled softly, scanning the disaster.

"Party," she explained succinctly.

"A party!" he snapped, eyes slitting ferociously.

"I turned thirty yesterday," she said. "And would you please stop shouting? My head is killing me."

Whatever Dev was going to say in response was cut off by another snore from the couch. He turned his head, clearly astounded.

In dreadful silence Tabitha listened as Ron Adams came awake with a muffled groan. Then, even as she watched, he sat up very slowly on the black couch, his dark eyes blinking balefully at the stranger with the ebony cane.

Dev, Tabitha realized, was absolutely thunderstruck. Even as that analysis was filtering through her confused mind, however, another realization dawned. As the shock in his rigid expression faded, it was being replaced by sheer rage.

Tabitha watched in morbid fascination as his steel gaze pinned her. Never had she seen this particular expression in a man's face. And she would happily live the rest of her life without ever witnessing it again. When he finally spoke, Dev's voice was as deadly as the secret sword in his cane.

"For the sake of formality let's run through a couple of quick explanations before I beat the living daylights out of you. *Who the hell is he?*"

Eight

He had never known this kind of sheer, masculine outrage in his life, Dev realized vaguely through the haze of his fury. This emotion wasn't the cold, lethal anger he had felt toward the men who had threatened Tabitha. It wasn't the fatalistic, brooding feeling he had known for a while after the realization that his marriage was faltering. It wasn't the wary animosity he had been experiencing toward Delaney lately.

It was the primitive male rage that engulfed a man when he found his woman in a compromising situation with another male. Dev had never truly experienced the sensation before, but his instincts told him exactly what it was when the emotion washed over him.

Damn it to hell! He hadn't meant the reunion with Tabby to go like this at all! During the entire trip to Port Townsend, he had tantalized himself with daydreams which all revolved around the image of having Tabby in his arms. He had wanted only to hear her purr again.

Now he wanted to see real fear in her eyes.

He wanted her quivering beneath the force of his rage.

He wanted her throwing herself at his feet and pleading for his understanding.

He wanted her so terrified of him that she would never again even think of waking up in the same room with another man; never even *look* at another man.

Especially not another man who only looked to be about twenty-five years old, by God!

But Tabitha wasn't shivering in terror or rushing to beg his forgiveness. She was holding her tousled head with both hands and glaring up at him in grim disgust. Dev had never seen her look at anyone in quite that way.

"If you don't stop shouting," she said with gentle dignity, "I'm going to have to ask you to leave."

"The hell you are! Who is he, Tabitha?"

"My name's Ron. Ron Adams." With grim determination Ron managed to get up off the couch. Cautiously he circled toward the door, leaving plenty of space between himself and the older man. "I, uh, was just on my way home. Honest. Bye, Tab. Great party. Happy birthday..."

Dev watched Ron's progress through evilly slitted eyes. At least this puppy was showing a bit of healthy fear. There was some satisfaction in that. "Don't rush off, Ron Adams. We have a few details to straighten out here."

"You leave him alone, Devlin Colter!' Tabitha hissed behind him.

Dev ignored her. He was having more success terrorizing Ron Adams, so he decided to pursue the task. "Just what the hell do you think you're doing spending the night with my woman?" He lowered his voice to that deceptively soft level that had been known to send chills down the spines of more resolute men than Ron Adams. When you are pushing forty and find yourself in a face-off with a twenty-five-year-old, you have a right to use a few tricks, Dev told himself.

"Look, Mr. Colter or whoever you are, I didn't know she was yours! That's the truth. Tell him, Tab!" Ron swung a pleading glance at Tabitha, urging her to defend him.

"I don't belong to anyone!" she stormed and then groaned as the sound of her own voice vibrated painfully through her head. "I wish you both would leave."

"What happened here last night?" Dev growled, paying no attention to her request. He concentrated on Ron Adams.

Ron put up a placating hand and shook his head. "Nothing," he declared earnestly. "I swear it. I came to Tab's birthday party with my sister and some friends. Had a few drinks. Then Tab and I started talking…" His voice trailed off weakly.

"Talking about what?" Dev prompted coldly.

"It's a bit fuzzy," Ron admitted morosely.

"The state of your memory might very well determine your physical condition when you leave this house." Dev waited with all the arrogant intimidation he could summon. It was a considerable amount and it had its effect.

"Animals," Ron remembered almost immediately. "That's all we talked about, wasn't it, Tab? Animals."

"Animals!" Dev thundered. He sent a ferocious glance at Tabitha. "*Animals!* You told *him* about the mating habits of medieval animals? How did you dare? You're only supposed to use that line on me! You have no right to go around discussing that sort of thing with every other male you come across! Tabby Graham, I really am going to beat you. I'm going to make certain you don't sit down for a week. Animals. I can't believe you actually went that far!"

"Why not?" she retorted spiritedly. "It worked so well on you I decided to try it out on another man. Field testing, so to speak."

"Field testing!" Dev realized he was nearly speechless with shock and outrage. He swung back to Ron Adams, who was almost safely out the door. "Listen to me, you young twerp. I'm going to let you go without breaking both of your legs only because I can see for myself that you didn't wind up in bed with Tabby. But if you ever come near her again, I won't be responsible for my actions, is that clear?"

"Very." Ron dashed gratefully for the door.

"And just forget everything you heard here about the mating habits of medieval animals. Understand?"

"Yes, sir," Ron assured him quickly, his hand on the doorknob. "Actually, I don't think we got past dragons. That's the truth. Scout's honor."

"You discussed dragons?" Dev asked ominously.

Tabitha had called *him* a dragon. "What did she tell you about dragons?"

"I...I'm not sure. It's all a bit vague," Ron explained hastily.

"Think hard," Dev advised grimly.

"Oh, Dev, will you cut it out? I'm sick and tired of all this male nonsense," Tabitha complained.

"Not until I hear what you told him about dragons." He saw Ron trying to gauge his chances of escaping through the front door and swung his cane up to bar his way. Intimidatingly he leaned toward the younger man. "Try very hard to remember, kid."

Ron swallowed awkwardly. "I, uh, think I asked her how dragons made love or something."

"And what did she tell you?"

Ron frowned in desperate concentration. "She, er, said something about them doing it magnificently, I think."

"Did she?" Dev smiled his best highwayman's smile and slowly lowered the cane. "She ought to know. She's had personal experience of the matter. I'm the dragon in question, you see."

Ron gulped. "I was beginning to get that impression. If you'll excuse me, I'll be on my way." He didn't wait for permission, moving down the steps with unsteady haste.

Dev watched his fleeing foe with savage satisfaction; then he turned back to confront Tabitha, who was sinking slowly down into a nearby chair, still clutching her head.

"What the hell did you want with a kid like that?" he muttered. "He must be a good five or six years younger than you!"

"It's the latest trend," she gritted, massaging her temples. "Younger men start looking very good when a woman hits thirty, you know."

"No, I didn't know! Damn it, Tabby, I'm about at the end of my patience. What kind of game are you playing, anyway?" He stalked closer, wanting to see a little terror in her. But she had closed her eyes in obvious suffering.

"The theory is that you can train them properly if you get them young," she explained. "Older men are rather set in their ways, you know. They're sneakier, less trustworthy."

"Tabby!"

"Yes sir, give me a younger man every time," she said, leaning her head back against the chair cushion. "They're cute. Eager to please, too."

"I'll bet!" Dev stalked forward another step, his knuckles whitening as he gripped the handle of the cane. "My God, Tabby, you're really walking the edge this morning, do you know that? The only thing saving your neck right now is the fact that I know you didn't actually go to bed with him!"

"How do you know?" she taunted.

Where was she getting the courage to defy him? Dev wondered furiously. Why wasn't she cowering and apologizing and generally pleading for mercy? Belatedly it occurred to him that no one had ever said tabby cats lacked guts. "Well, for starters, you're both still fully dressed," he mocked brutally. "You've even got your pantyhose on. Most women who've spent the night in wild abandon with a young stud lose their pantyhose somewhere along the way."

"Oh." Tabitha opened her eyes and glared balefully down at her stocking-shod feet. "I always said you were very observant," she sighed.

"Furthermore, it's obvious he slept on that small sofa. There really isn't room for two on it. And it looks like you slept on the other one. One of your shoes is still on the cushion," he added derisively, flicking a scathing glance at the article of furniture in question.

"What good eyes you have, grandpa."

"Don't call me grandpa!" Dev roared. It was the last straw. He dropped the cane and closed his hands around Tabitha's shoulders, hauling her unceremoniously to her feet. "I may not be twenty-five any longer, but I'm willing to bet I can get further than that young puppy did last night! Shall we find out, Tabby? Let's see if a few years of experience make any difference! If you'd spent the night with me, you wouldn't have awakened this morning still wearing your pantyhose!"

"Maybe I'm not interested in your kind of experience," she shot back bravely. "Maybe I don't want a man who lies to me. Who makes me think he's someone he's not. A man who deliberately leads me to believe he's gentle and vulnerable and shy. A man who makes me think he's a lot like me! Who *deceives* me!"

"Tabby, I didn't deceive you!" Oh, God, he'd been afraid of this. How was he going to fight the accusations? How could he explain why he'd been another man when he was with her?

"Yes, you did. You go around cutting throats for a living with that…that sword you carry. You're not a travel agent!" she exclaimed furiously.

"Yes, I am a travel agent, damn it!'

"You see? Lying is second nature to you now that you're nearly forty! You've probably been doing it so long you don't know how to tell the truth! Are you going to try to pretend you're the emotionally sensitive and vulnerable man I thought I met on that ship?"

"Damn right, I am!" he blazed.

"Hah! It's too late, Dev. I've seen you in action. I know you were only using me. I made a nice cover for you, didn't I? Who would expect a real, live secret agent to hang around with a woman like me?"

"What makes you think you know what I do for a living?"

"Steve Waverly told me all about it during that pleasant little wait I had while you figured out I was never coming back from the rest room!" she fumed, remembering.

Dev sucked in his breath. "Did he?"

Tabitha frowned even more severely. "Why are you turning pale?"

"Probably because I'm realizing that he meant to kill you. He would never have told you anything if he'd intended to let you go free. I should have cut the bastard's throat."

"You see? That's exactly what I mean! An emotionally sensitive, gentle, vulnerable man doesn't go around threatening to cut other men's throats!"

"Tabby, you're going to listen to me if I have to beat the facts into you!" He gave her a small shake and saw her eyes widen abruptly. But it wasn't with fear. "Tabby?" he prodded with sudden anxiety. "What's wrong?"

"I think I'm going to be sick," she announced gravely.

"Oh, hell."

Her hand flew to her mouth. "Go away, Dev. Just go *away!*" She tried to twist free of his grip but Dev only gathered her closer.

"Which way is the bathroom?" he demanded. When she gestured mutely, he started purposefully forward. It was a little awkward holding onto her and balancing himself without the cane but they made it in time. Barely. He held her gently as she leaned over the porcelain bowl, and wiped her face with a damp cloth afterward. "Feel better?" he asked softly when it was all over. She was shivering now, not with fear but from reaction to being so ill.

Tabitha nodded but for the first time that morning her eyes slid away from his and Dev realized she was embarrassed. "Thank you," she said very formally.

"Come on, you need a good hot shower and a decent breakfast." Holding her against his side, he industriously began getting her out of the black dress she was wearing.

"No, Dev, please!"

But she was really too weak to resist him, although she slapped futilely at his hands. When he simply ignored her small struggles, she appeared to give up and submitted meekly to being undressed and put into a hot shower.

"You didn't wear a bra last night!" he accused as he folded the clothing she had been wearing.

"Haven't worn one for several days," she retorted from inside the shower, where she was leaning precariously against the tile wall. "It's part of the new me."

"You're only supposed to go without one when you're trying to seduce me," he flung back in annoyance. "Damn it, forget it. We'll discuss this later. How's your head?"

"Hurts."

"Here, I found this in your medicine cupboard." He opened the shower door and pushed two tablets into her mouth. Then he handed her a glass of water and watched while she obediently swallowed them. "Ever had a hangover before?" he demanded critically, surveying her gently rounded body with a kind of professional interest. She was so soft and inviting. He'd been dreaming about her for days. It was hard to believe he had her back within reach finally.

When she became aware of his scrutiny her hands went up to cover her full breasts and she deliberately turned her back to him. "No," she mumbled. "I've never had a hangover."

"What the hell got into you, Tabby?" he groaned, his eyes on the curve of her backside. Unable to resist, he put out a hand and shaped the wet, tantalizing globe of her buttock. She flinched and stepped nervously out of reach but continued to keep her back to him.

"I told you, it was my birthday party. I decided to make a new start. I was going to be a phoenix rising from the ashes."

Dev set his teeth and shut the shower door. He really didn't have the heart to grill her when she looked so washed out and weak. Later, he vowed, as he selected a huge towel from the closet. Later he would finish reading her the riot act. He glanced down at the towel and saw that it was embroidered with the head of a unicorn.

Inside the shower Tabitha turned her face up to the pounding water and tried to think. She really was feeling much better but it seemed safer somehow to go on pretending to be quite weak. Ever since she had warned him she was going to be sick, Dev had been treating her with great gentleness. His touch had been reassuring and kind; she had to admire a man who could deal with a sick woman. Most men were far too squeamish to handle that kind of scene.

Of course, a man who went around slicing people with his sword cane probably didn't have a squeamish attitude toward much of anything, she told herself violently. On the other hand, you wouldn't expect such a man to be quite so gentle with someone who was genuinely ill, either.

Well, she couldn't stay in the shower forever. Sooner or later she was going to have to emerge and find out exactly what Devlin Colter was doing in Port Townsend. With a groan she turned off the taps and opened the door a couple of inches. "Would you please hand me a towel?" she asked very politely.

"Come on out, honey. I'll dry you off."

"No, Dev, really, I'd rather..." But he was already pushing open the door and hauling her carefully out. There was nothing else she could do except stand quietly while he began to rub her down. He stood with his legs braced a couple of feet apart, and she realized that was the way he balanced himself when he didn't have his cane.

His hands on her body were intimate but they made

no demands. It was the touch of a lover who wasn't intent on making love just at the moment but who still felt possessive. Tabitha shivered.

"Relax," he growled. "I'm not going to hurt you."

"You were threatening to beat me," she reminded him.

"I still might, but not until you're feeling more normal," he grunted. "There." He folded the towel around her breasts, his hands lingering on the full curves for a few seconds. "You go get dressed while I see about something for breakfast."

Tabitha nodded, turning gratefully away to make her escape.

"And this time put on a bra!'

She emerged cautiously from the bedroom after delaying the inevitable as long as possible. Feeling more normal in a pair of jeans and a loose turquoise and yellow striped long-sleeved top, she peered around the corner into the kitchen before entering. Dev had collected his cane again, hooking it over a kitchen chair while he worked industriously on an omelette.

"Come on in, I'm not going to bite you. Not yet, at any rate."

"I'm not afraid of you," she muttered. Deliberately she sauntered into the room and sat down with what she hoped was a careless sprawl.

"Maybe you should be," he advised laconically. "Finding you standing amid the aftermath of an orgy has not put me into a good frame of mind."

"It wasn't an orgy! I keep telling you, it was my birthday party."

"What did you do? Invite every young male in town so you could pick and choose among them?"

"I invited everyone I knew. Period. Some of that crowd included young men, yes." She lifted her chin defiantly. "I decided to take a few lessons from my recent cruise."

"Decided to try your hand at seducing everything in trousers?"

"Why not? I had so much luck with you!" she tossed back lightly.

"Really? If you were getting so good at that sort of thing, what went wrong last night?"

Tabitha winced. "That's none of your business."

Dev glanced up, one brow rising curiously. He didn't seem so angry now, Tabitha decided. Why not? Or perhaps a better question would be, why had he been so angry in the first place? Why was he even here, come to that?

"Did you really tell that kid that I made love magnificently?" he drawled, sliding the omelette out of the pan and onto a plate.

"We were discussing dragons at the time, not you!"

"The hell you were," he contradicted gently, setting the food in front of her. "I'm the only dragon whose mating habits you're familiar with. You told me yourself the bestiaries don't have much information on the topic."

"Dev, why are you here?" she demanded roughly, eyeing the omelette with caution. Was her stomach really steady enough for food now?

"I'm here to collect you, tabby cat." He poured himself a cup of coffee, shoved aside a tray of leftover cheese sticks which was sitting on his side of the table and sat down.

Tabitha heard the resolute note in his voice and bit nervously into a forkful of omelette. She would not let him put her off stride again. "Why?"

"Because I want you," he said simply and then leaned back to sip his coffee just as if he were discussing the weather. He watched her intently over the rim of the cup. "And I need you, Tabby."

"Need me! Men who carry swords in their canes don't need people like me!"

"Yes, we do. I do, at any rate," he countered softly. "You were falling in love with me on that ship, weren't you, Tabby?"

She flinched. "What if I was? I got over it in a hurry just as soon as I found out you had lied to me and used me."

"I didn't use you! What exactly did Waverly tell you?"

Her eyes narrowed. "That you were a government agent and that you had made a routine pickup for your department on St. Regis. He had decided to relieve you of the film you collected in that alley. What did happen in that alley, Dev? Who was it you left stuffed into the trash container?"

Dev hesitated and then lifted one shoulder indifferently. "Someone who tried to intercept the film."

"That's why you were all beaten up?"

Dev nodded once, watching her warily. "I very nearly lost, Tabby. With a little less luck it would have been me who got stuffed into that trash bin. I'm getting too old for that kind of work. I'd been telling Delaney that for two years."

"Who's Delaney?"

"Washington, D.C. type. You know, I told you how they were. Hard and cold. I used to work for him until my accident."

"Oh, yes, the famous accident. Did you lie to me about that, too? Were you really in a car wreck?" she demanded scathingly.

"Tabby..."

"Answer me!"

"Not exactly," he grated harshly. "On my last assignment for Delaney I had a little trouble with a couple of terrorists I'd been told to stop. They nearly stopped me, instead."

Tabitha winced in spite of her resolution to remain implacable. "Oh, Dev! What happened?" Her eyes betrayed the flash of concern she was trying to stifle.

"Against my better judgment, against my *instincts,* I agreed to meet with an informer. The guy was supposed to be supplying us with reliable information. The night I turned up for the rendezvous he turned up with the two guys I'd been trailing. I wound up with a bullet in my left knee and a few other assorted bruises."

"What happened to them?" she asked quietly.

"One escaped. The informer. A friend of mine got him for me later."

"And the two terrorists?" she whispered.

"Tabby..." he began.

"What happened to them?"

Dev sighed. "I shot both of them. There, are you satisfied? It's what you wanted to hear, isn't it? That I'm a violent sort of man? Capable of shooting people or slicing their throats? Tabby, that rendezvous was miles from the nearest town. I nearly bled to death before I got help. As it was, the doctor wanted to amputate my leg. I didn't dare let him give me any anesthetic for fear he'd go ahead and cut it off while I was under! I had to fight to keep him from doing anything drastic until Delaney got me to a decent hospital!''

"My God, Dev," she breathed, horrified at the bleak, remembered pain she could see in his silver eyes. "I didn't realize..."

"Afterward I told Delaney I'd had enough. I wanted out. He said all I needed was a few months to recover and I'd be chomping at the bit to get back to work. Tabby, I really am a travel agent. I opened the business after I got back on my feet. I had done a lot of traveling in my work for Delaney's department, and I figured if there was one thing I knew about, it was globe-trotting. I've been working hard for months to establish the business." Dev broke off and sighed. "Then Delaney contacted me a few weeks ago and asked if I'd make the pickup for him on St. Regis. The film was important, he said. It's got something to do with laser technology. Delaney thought it would be simple for me to take the cruise under my legitimate cover as a travel agent. And I..."

"You what?" she prompted grimly.

"Hell, I don't know. Maybe I was curious to see if he was right. He claimed that once I got my feet wet again, I'd be ready to go back to work on a full-time basis. I don't know, Tabby. I only knew that something was missing in my life. I was putting the travel business together all right, but it wasn't enough. I wasn't satisfied. And Delaney had once been a good friend. I agreed to do the job for him. But I started regretting it as soon as I got on the boat. I knew I was no longer cut out for that kind of work. Then you came to my rescue in that alley, and I began to realize what it was that had been missing in my life. It wasn't the excitement of working for Delaney. It was having someone care for me and love me and shower me with attention. What I really wanted was a sweet, gentle tabby cat who would curl up in my lap and make love to me.''

Tabitha felt the warm flush rise in her face as she steadfastly refused to meet his glance. ''I'm not going to play tabby cat any longer, Dev. I felt like an absolute fool the last time. You used me. Oh, maybe not as a cover for your work, although I have a hunch it suited your purposes to have me hanging around for that reason, too. But you took advantage of my unquestioning assumption that you and I were two of a kind. You more or less lied to me, Dev. When I think of what an idiot I was...''

''You weren't an idiot!''

Her head came up swiftly. ''Oh, yes, I was. Do you know how I feel every time I think back to that night when I supposedly seduced you? I actually thought you were too shy to make the first move, did you know that? I thought you were such a sensitive man you were terrified of forcing yourself on me!''

''I *was* terrified of doing exactly that,'' he cut in savagely. ''I knew you'd run for cover if I came on too strong. It seemed safest to let you set the pace until you felt comfortable with me.''

''You mean you decided to let me wander so far into the trap I wouldn't be able to escape when you shut the door! But I'm out now, Dev, and I'm a different woman from the one who wandered so blithely inside. I learned a lot on that cruise!"

"Don't ever forget that what you learned, you learned from me!" he snapped abruptly. "I know what the problem is here: you've discovered the passionate side of your nature and now you're determined to find out what you've been missing. You want to be free to explore the side of you that's been locked up all these years. But if you think I set that side of you free just so you could turn around and throw yourself at every young stud who comes along, you're out of your head! You belong to me now!" The coffee cup crashed down onto the table as Dev straightened and leaned forward in his chair. His hard face was set in fierce lines as he challenged her.

"I'm a changed woman and there's nothing you can do about it! I'll live my life exactly the way I want to live it, and if I happen to feel like running around with nice young men like Ron Adams, I will, by God!"

With an obvious effort of will Dev brought his voice back under control. "Tabby, Tabby, I didn't come here to yell at you."

"No? You're doing a pretty good job of it."

He groaned in exasperation. "Honey, my instincts all tell me there's no way you could have changed fundamentally in the few days that have passed since you left the cruise. That's the real reason I let you and your young friend off so lightly this morning. I know damn well that whatever happened here last night, you weren't really very likely to have gotten yourself involved in a genuine one-night stand!"

"Why not? I did with you!"

"I'm different," he told her evenly.

She blinked owlishly, not trusting his expression of utter conviction. "What makes you so sure of that?"

"Instinct."

"Oh, shut up!" She reached for her coffee cup, glowering down at the dark brew.

"It's true. Tabby, I survived for years on my instincts. Let me show you that they can be trusted. Let me show you that you really do belong to me."

Tabitha eyed him uneasily. "You might trust your instincts, Dev, but I don't trust you."

A flicker of pain flashed briefly in his eyes, but his voice was steady as he said quietly, "Okay, so you don't trust me. Are you going to admit you're afraid of me?"

"I'm not afraid of you," she informed him aloofly.

He gazed at her consideringly. "What if I told you I came here to return the favor you did me on board ship?"

"You mean repay me for getting you out of that alley?"

He smiled slightly, a small, wicked twist of his mouth that stirred the delicate hair at the nape of her neck. "I meant the favor you did when you seduced me. One good turn deserves another, Tabby. It strikes me that you've never really been properly seduced. Your ex-husband obviously didn't know how, and lately you've been making all the moves yourself. It's time you learned one of the fundamental pleasures of life, honey, and who better to learn it from than the man who's going to marry you?"

Nine

It wasn't the wicked smile or the blunt masculine aggression. It wasn't the fact that Dev had actually spoken of marriage. It wasn't even because she had been feeling uncomfortably hung over and was therefore in a weakened condition.

None of those had anything to do with the decision she had made, Tabitha thought resentfully as she whipped a feather duster over a shelf of books at The Manticore. No, she had accepted the date with Dev because of the flash of grim desperation she had seen in his silver eyes. It was that strange urgency coupled with a mental image of him nearly bleeding to death on some lonely road two years previously that had done her in, Tabitha knew.

Damn! What was the matter with her? Why hadn't she simply kicked him out of the house? Morosely she dusted a shelf of science fiction books and then abandoned the task altogether in favor of sitting on her stool behind the counter. The shop was empty at the moment; there was no distraction to stop her from dwelling on her own stupidity. The conversation at the breakfast table that morning kept replaying through her mind.

"Marry you! Not a chance!" she'd choked.

"You're afraid of me."

"I am not afraid of you," she'd gritted, meaning every word.

"Then prove it by having dinner with me, tonight."

"Dev, this is ridiculous. First you were talking about marriage and now you're discussing dinner!'

"One step at a time. Tabby, at least come out to dinner with me," he'd ordered softly. It was then that she'd seen the flash of urgent need in his eyes and her resolve had faltered. In the end she'd grumblingly agreed to have dinner with him, and now she could only sit, chin in hand, and berate herself.

Because she was in love with him.

She'd known that the moment she'd opened the door this morning and found him on the step. No, Tabitha corrected herself dismally, she'd known it last night when she'd looked down at the dragon in the carpet and realized through the haze of alcohol that she had no business telling Ron Adams about the medieval version of the birds and the bees. The only man she wanted to seduce was Dev Colter.

Travel agent! Likely story. But what the devil was he doing here in Port Townsend if he wasn't telling her the essential truth? If he'd only been using her on board the ship would he have bothered tracking her

down now? And what was the meaning of that desperate determination she had sensed in him?

What if Dev Colter were now telling her the truth?
He was the man she had rescued from that alley on
St. Regis, after all, even if she hadn't known the real
reason for his being there. One thing hadn't altered:
when she had come across him in that brick alley he
had needed her badly and she had taken care of him.
She would have done the same even had she known
he'd left his assailant behind stuffed in a trash bin.
There was no way she could have turned from him
in that moment.

Now here he was in Port Townsend telling her that
he needed her again. He wasn't bruised and bleeding
this time, but she had seen pain in his eyes and she
wasn't at all sure she would be able to turn from him
this go round, either. He was an annoying, demanding, somewhat deceptive sort of beast, but he was *her*
beast, her very own dragon.

Tabitha sighed and reflected on that thought for a
moment. Something about having rescued a man and
then seducing him gave a woman a very possessive
sort of feeling toward him. And the feeling must be
somewhat mutual because she'd seen the aggressive
fury in those silver eyes this morning when Dev had
found Ron Adams amid the shambles of her birthday
party.

She shuddered as the shop door opened. It occurred
to Tabitha that she was very glad Dev's "instincts"
had told him nothing serious had happened between
herself and Ron. She didn't like to think of what he
might have done if he'd felt the younger man had
poached on his territory.

"Good morning, Tab," Sandra Adams called as she came through the door. "Just wanted to stop by and tell you what a fantastic party that was last night! Had a great time. Jim is absolutely the most interesting fisherman I've ever encountered. The strong, silent type, you know. At one with the sea and the storms," she continued melodramatically, "a part of the primeval forces of nature, etcetera, etcetera. Love those primeval forces. And what the heck did you do to my little brother, by the way?"

Tabitha grimaced as her friend lounged against the counter and regarded her with amused eyes. "He fell asleep on my couch."

"And awakened to the roar of a dragon, according to him." Sandra grinned. "Naturally I hastened over to hear more about the beast." The shop door chimed just as she spoke and automatically Sandra glanced over her shoulder to see who was entering. "Don't tell me. The dragon, right?"

Dev arched a dark brow as he walked in, carrying two Styrofoam cups of coffee carefully cradled in one large hand. He used the ebony cane to shove the door shut behind him. "My reputation seems to have preceded me," he mocked dryly.

"No wonder my little brother was overwhelmed. You must have a good fifteen years on the lad."

"Don't remind me," Dev growled feelingly. "You're the kid's sister?"

"Sandra, this is Devlin Colter." Tabitha hastily made introductions, aware of a strange feeling of wariness as she saw the speculative gleam in Sandra's eyes. The hint of jealousy vanished almost at once, however, because Dev totally ignored the other woman's incipient interest. Just as on the ship, he seemed oblivious to the curiosity or the speculation in the eyes of any woman but Tabitha. Tabitha knew a measure of happy satisfaction which she instantly tried to squelch. "Dev and I met on the cruise," she explained weakly.

"It must have been some cruise," Sandra observed cheerfully to Dev. "Tab came back a changed woman."

"Not really," Dev murmured, handing a cup of coffee to Tabitha. He smiled gently as she avoided his gaze by hurriedly snapping open the plastic lid. "She just learned a little more about herself, that's all."

"Sandy's quite right," Tabitha announced defiantly as she swallowed a large sip of steaming coffee. "I'm changed."

Dev just smiled again and peeled off his own lid.

"Well, if the two of you will excuse me, I've got some grocery shopping to do," Sandra declared brightly, heading for the door. "I see that little dress shop next to you has closed, Tab. Going to lease the space and expand The Manticore?"

"I haven't decided yet," Tabitha said honestly, her mind not really on the subject. "I'm thinking about it. Goodbye, Sandy. Thanks for coming to the party last night."

"My pleasure, believe me!" Sandra shut the door behind her with a chuckle.

"Resigned yourself to having dinner with me tonight?" Dev asked mildly as he glanced curiously around the shop.

"Dev, I want you to understand that this is only a

dinner date, nothing more," she told him severely. "Is that very clear?"

"Meaning I'm not supposed to seduce you?"

"Meaning we can have a pleasant evening if you behave yourself! I won't be pushed, Dev. I have a lot of serious thinking to do about us, and I don't want you trying to maneuver me."

"Yes, ma'am," he agreed humbly. "Let's just say we're getting together for the sake of old times. How's that?"

Tabitha glared at him suspiciously, declining to answer that one.

She was still eyeing Dev suspiciously that night as she sat across from him in the charming harbor-front restaurant he had chosen. But she felt reasonably able to hold her own that evening. Dev had been the model of gentlemanly behavior since the moment he had arrived at her door in a subdued, dark, linen jacket and trousers. She herself was wearing a white knit dress trimmed in black.

His refined manners had reestablished her own sense of equilibrium but she knew him much better now than she had on the ship, and Tabitha's innate caution was still in effect as they ordered lobster soufflés and celery, radish and olive salads.

"Stop worrying," Dev drawled softly. "I'll warn you when the seduction is about to start. Just as you warned me."

Her brows drew together in a fierce line. "What do you mean by that?"

"Well, first there was that charming kiss on deck in the moonlight," he mused. "I got my hopes up, but nothing came of it that night. The morning you met me at your cabin door wearing that loose, little cotton thing without any bra on underneath, I told myself that there was still a chance.''

"You were laughing at me," she accused tightly. "All the time. God, I feel like such a fool."

"Tabby, I wasn't laughing at you," he said evenly. "I wanted you to make love to me so badly, and I was so afraid you'd lose your nerve."

"Too bad I didn't."

"Don't say that. The night you seduced me was the most memorable evening of my life," he said wistfully. "I wouldn't trade that memory for anything on earth."

She regarded him skeptically, desperately wanting to believe their night together had meant that much to him. "I'm sure you've enjoyed many similar evenings."

"I've never spent another evening like that one," he said simply.

"Hah!"

"It's true," he said. "I've never had another woman really make love to me. And you were making love that night, weren't you? Not just having a fling with me?"

"You've been married!" she protested. "Or was that a lie, too?"

A flare of anger at the accusation lit his eyes and then was firmly repressed. "I was married," he confirmed. "But she was in love with the image of my job, not with me. That's why she left me, Tabby, after I nearly lost my leg. She wanted a James Bond, and I was only willing to give her a mundane businessman."

Tabitha bit her lip as a pang of sympathy welled up inside. She knew what it was to be married for all the wrong reasons. "Is that the truth?"

"Tabby, I've always told you the truth except about the reason I was in that alley on St. Regis. Frankly, I wasn't free to tell you those facts. Not until you found them out the hard way by having a gun held to your head. I felt so damn guilty about getting you into that mess, honey. It was all my fault. Afterward I couldn't think of anything else but finding you and straightening everything out between us. But you were gone when I got back to the ship."

"I couldn't stand the thought of facing you after that. I was so angry. And I felt like an idiot for having mistaken a tough, hard-bitten secret agent type for a mild-mannered, gentlemanly travel agent who was…"

"…vulnerable, sensitive and shy. I know," he finished wryly. "But, honey, that's exactly what I am. Well, maybe I'm not particularly *shy*," he conceded honestly, "but I am vulnerable and sensitive and…"

"Dev, I think we'd better go on to another topic before I pour this excellent Chardonnay over your head," Tabitha threatened violently.

His mouth hardened and for an instant she thought he might override her demand. But he didn't. Instead he obediently changed the subject, asking her about Port Townsend and how long she'd had The Manticore. In a surprisingly short time Tabitha found herself chatting freely once again, just as she had on the ship. Slowly Tabitha began to relax. In spite of all the uncertainty, this was where she wanted to be and

this was the man she wanted to be with tonight. She
loved Dev Colter.

Dev watched her gradual relaxation with a sense of
gratification. It was working. She was rapidly turning
back into the charming, soft, feminine creature she
had been on board ship. He was managing to undo
some of the damage. She was seeing him now less
and less as the ruthless agent she had watched in action on the island and more as the ordinary, non-
threatening businessman he truly was. Dev began to
relax a little himself. He hadn't realized just how
tense he had been for the past few days.

It had taken careful planning and thought to decide
just when to pursue her to Port Townsend. His instincts had warned him to give her a little time to get
over her hurt and resentment. But his instincts had
very nearly kept him away too long, he thought in
annoyance. Walking in on that little morning-after
scene today had told him that much. How did the
tabby cat dare play around with her newfound self-
confidence?

Grimly Dev tamped down the rising irritation. He
had arrived in time. There would be no repeat per-
formance. Tabitha would not be practicing her unique
seduction techniques on anyone except him from now
on! Belatedly he realized that something of his determination must be showing in his face, because she
was eyeing him a little warily from the other side of
the table. Dev smiled blandly.

"Have some more wine, Tabby. It's very good. I
had no idea your northwestern wines were becoming
so competitive with California's."

The caution in her eyes eased once again and she

went on to tell him about the thriving wine industries in Washington and Oregon. Dev listened attentively. He found her so soothing to listen to, he realized vaguely. Soothing and charming and sweetly exciting.

By the time he drove her home after dinner Dev was feeling quite certain of his progress. Tabitha, he decided happily, was very nearly back in his lap. The wariness in her had diminished to almost nothing and the warmth was back in her sherry-colored eyes. She hadn't resisted at all when he'd taken her hand to walk her back out to the car, and he felt quite sure she wouldn't resist when he took her in his arms later. Once he had her safely in his arms, he told himself, everything would be perfect.

He was right up to a point.

"Is this the beginning of the seduction?" she asked with grave interest as he closed the door of her cottage behind him, hooked his cane over the knob and started to pull her close.

He smiled sensually down at her, inhaling the tantalizing, female fragrance of her hair and skin. "I do believe it is," he murmured. Actually, the seduction had been going on all evening, but if she didn't realize it, who was he to tell her? His smile widened, lighting his eyes as he traced the line of her cheek with his finger. God, it was good to be touching her again. So very, very good. Dev sighed softly and bent his head to taste her lips.

"Well, in that case, this is where I say good night," Tabitha declared firmly and planted both of her small hands against his chest.

Dev blinked in surprise. "What?"

"You heard me. Good night, Dev. I had a lovely

evening.'' She smiled a bit too brilliantly for his liking.

"Tabby...!"

"You have to go now, Dev, because I haven't made up my mind about us yet. I still have a lot of thinking to do," she explained very kindly.

He bit back the rather violent four-letter word which came to his lips. He wouldn't push her. She was almost back where she belonged, and he could afford to wait until she came the rest of the way of her own free will. He had the rest of his life to think about. Surely he could hold off for another night or so before securing his future? Where was all that much-vaunted patience he had learned through the years? With a supreme effort of will he summoned another smile and bent down to brush her lips.

"Thank you for trusting me enough to come out with me tonight, Tabby," he murmured, injecting as much humble gratitude into his voice as he could manage under the circumstances. "I'll call you in the morning."

For just an instant she hesitated, a worried expression coming to her eyes. "Have you got a place to stay?" she asked a little gruffly.

It took fortitude, but Dev succeeded in passing up the obvious opportunity. What would she do if he said he had nowhere to go tonight? Offer him a couch? He'd never know because he had already made up his mind to go on playing the gentleman. "I'm staying in one of those old Victorian monstrosities someone has converted into a bed and breakfast place. Don't worry about me, Tabby."

"I won't," she agreed with alacrity. "Good night, Dev."

"Good night, Tabby." He hesitated wistfully, but could think of no further excuse for staying. Without another word he grasped his cane and let himself out the door. Patience, he instructed himself grimly. You're supposed to be good at waiting. Just give her a little more time and she'll be yours. The woman's in love with you. She had to be in love with him, damn it!

Dev was still consoling himself with that promise four days later as he dressed for yet another evening out with Tabitha Graham. She had to be in love with him; he refused to consider any other possibility. But why the hell was she insisting on keeping him at arm's length?

With a savage twist, he finished knotting his tie and reached for the jacket hanging on the chair. Automatically he checked for his keys and wallet and then headed for the door of the room. Was she playing some kind of game with him? Punishing him perhaps for not being the man she had wanted him to be on board ship? Or was she just uncertain of herself?

If it was uncertainty, he had to decide how long to let it go on before putting a stop to this nonsense. If she was playing games, he would damn well put a halt to them as fast as possible. And if she was trying to punish him... He winced at the thought. Perhaps he deserved it. Down in the tiny parking lot of the old Victorian Inn he slammed the rental car in gear and pulled out into the street, heading for Tabby's little cottage. One way or another he had to find out what she thought she was doing, and then he had to put a stop to it. His patience was nearly gone and all his instincts were coming uneasily alive in warning.

Warning of what? That Tabby might really have changed? That she might have become a harder, slightly vicious little cat? No, he didn't want to believe that. He couldn't believe it. He had seen the gentle compassion in her eyes too often during the past few days. She couldn't have changed so fundamentally.

So why was he feeling that sense of restless unease again tonight? God, he hated these prickly sensations of impending disaster, even if he did occasionally owe his life to their warning signals.

Tonight was the night, he decided grimly, his hands tightening on the steering wheel. Tonight he would settle matters once and for all. Tabitha belonged in his bed, and the sooner she rediscovered that fact, the better for both of them. This fencing game she was playing with him was going to drive him out of his mind. He had been so sure that she'd surrender right away. After all, she *loved* him.

God help him if she didn't.

With admirable self-mastery, he hid the growing sense of desperation he was feeling as he took Tabitha out on yet another dinner date. This time she had recommended an expensive French restaurant housed in yet another of the restored Victorian homes for which the town was famed.

"One of the best examples of Victorian architecture north of San Francisco," Tabitha had told him proudly as she had taken him through Port Townsend the day before. "We've been designated a National Historic District, you know."

"I didn't know," he'd murmured, wondering what she would do if he just dragged her down onto the grass of the nearest park and made love to her right then and there. But of course he hadn't. He was a gentleman.

But tonight urgent instincts were overriding the refined, sensitive gentleman in him. Dev knew he had to get things settled. His nerves, once thought by many to be made of steel, weren't going to survive this torture much longer.

"A new piece of jewelry?" he asked politely halfway through the shrimp in cognac cream sauce that they had both ordered. He peered at the necklace more closely.

"Do you like it?" she asked excitedly. "A friend of mine made it. It's a centaur. Half man, half horse. Supposed to be a very lusty animal."

As soon as the words were out of her mouth Dev knew she regretted having dragged the topic of sex into the conversation. He saw the pink tinge in her cheeks and smiled to himself. At least the concept of sex was also on her mind!

"Lustier than dragons?" he asked innocently.

She coughed and reached for her wineglass. "Well, as I told you, no one seems to know much about the sex habits of dragons…"

"Except you," he reminded her bluntly.

"If you don't mind, I would prefer to change the subject," she replied loftily.

"Whatever you say, honey."

She could change the subject, but damned if he was going to let her get away with forgetting about sex altogether! Tonight he was going to make love to her and still these nagging, restless prickles of warning which had been haunting him all afternoon. He needed the reassurance now of having her back in his arms.

"Will you come in for a nightcap?" she asked easily at the door later on that evening. She'd invited him in for the preceding two nights and had found him simple enough to get rid of afterward, Dev thought wryly. He hadn't yet given her a reason to think tonight would be different.

"Thank you, Tabby. I'd like that."

He watched her disappear into the kitchen and then he carefully lowered himself to one knee in front of the fireplace and began building a blaze on the hearth. He was getting to his feet, using the cane as a lever, when she returned a short time later with two brandies in snifters. Dev winced and then smiled bravely.

"What's the matter?" she demanded in immediate concern. "Is your leg bothering you tonight?" Hastily she set down the brandies and came forward to help him to the couch.

"A little. It'll be fine in a moment. All that walking around town yesterday afternoon might have been a bit much."

"I shouldn't have run you all over the place looking at Victorian houses," she chastised herself, assisting him onto the couch. "Here, have some brandy."

Gratefully he accepted the snifter. She sat down beside him and frowned intently until he took a sip and then assured her his leg was better in its present position. "I'll just have to stay off of it for a few minutes. It'll be fine by the time I leave."

Since he didn't intend to leave until morning that would probably not be a lie, he told himself. A night in Tabby's bed would be more than enough medicine to soothe the slight, aching twinge he had experienced when he'd used the cane to get to his feet a moment ago. Then he noticed she was still frowning.

"That's something I want to talk to you about, Dev," she began very precisely.

"Leaving?" He tensed but hid the reaction with a faint whimsical smile. "Already? I haven't even finished my brandy."

"I don't mean tonight," she countered carefully. "I mean for good. What exactly are your plans, Dev? How long will you be staying here in Port Townsend?" She raised her eyes determinedly to meet his quizzical gaze.

He took a long breath and let it out slowly. "For good, I think."

"For good!" The brandy sloshed precariously in her snifter as she stared at him. "What are you talking about?"

"About opening a travel agency in that shop next to yours, the one that's going to be for lease soon," he told her flatly, holding her eyes with his own. "About moving permanently from Houston to Port Townsend. About marrying you."

He watched the expressions chase each other across her sensitive features. She hadn't been prepared for anything quite so blatant tonight and it showed. Well, the waiting was over as far as he was concerned. There was no reason not to be blunt.

"But, Dev, surely you aren't prepared to make a major decision like moving to Port Townsend on the spur of the moment! I mean, there are so many things to consider...."

"I can't really see you in Houston," he remarked blandly. "So I think I will have to be the one to do the moving. You're not a Houston type, you see, just as you aren't a Washington, D.C. type."

The snifter in her hand trembled slightly. "And what type are you?" she asked anxiously.

"The type who was born to run a travel agency in Port Townsend. Tabby, why have you been keeping me at a distance for the past few days?" he asked with a hint of the aggression he had been repressing all evening.

She licked her lips cautiously. He could read the sudden wariness in her eyes. She knew he had just taken over the direction of the evening, and she wasn't at all sure how to stop him. "I've told you, Dev, I don't intend to allow you to rush me into anything. I don't want to make another mistake the way I did on the ship. I want to be sure of what I'm doing this time."

He stared broodingly down into the swirling brandy in his glass. "Time just ran out on you, Tabby. I'm staying the night."

"No."

Dev glanced up because the small word had been only a breath of sound on her lips. She was staring at him as if he really were a dragon and herself an unfortunate princess trapped in his lair. There was nothing to be gained by trying to reassure her. He was determined to be honest. He didn't want any more accusations of deception aimed at him.

"Yes." He set down his snifter and reached for her.

The paralysis which seemed to have her in its grip broke just as he wrapped his hand around the nape of her neck. The brandy in her snifter sloshed as she tried to evade him and her eyes opened wide with outrage and something else. Something Dev hoped very much was excitement.

"Damn it, Dev, you're not going to push me around!"

He held her at the back of her neck and carefully removed the brandy glass from her fingers. "I told you I'd give you fair warning of when the actual seduction started. Well, this is it, tabby cat. I'm going to hold you in my arms here in front of the fire and stroke you until you purr for me. I'm going to make love to you, Tabby Graham; seduce you until you can't think of anything else except making love back to me."

Dev knew that although the words were meant to sound sensual there was an underlying hardness he couldn't filter out. He was too desperate, too set on possessing her once more to infuse a mellow, seductive quality into his voice. Perhaps if he'd managed that feat he wouldn't have suddenly found himself tangling with a hellcat.

Tabby seemed to explode in his grasp, wrenching furiously away from his restraining fingers.

"Let me go, Dev, or so help me, I'll…" She didn't finish the sentence, wriggling fiercely out from under his hand and leaping to her feet.

If he didn't catch her quickly she would have an advantage over him, Dev acknowledged. His weak leg made running next to impossible and without the cane as an aid he would have a hell of a job catching her before she fled out into the street. The ebony stick lay a couple of feet away, just out of reach.

"Tabby, come here," he rasped harshly as she began to back toward the fire. There was a flame in her brown eyes which was as golden as that on the hearth; she shook her head violently. "Tabby," he repeated softly, "you know you don't want to run from me. I'm the man who helped you find out just how passionate you really are. Come here, sweetheart, it's time you repeated the experience."

Hell. He was handling this very badly, Dev realized grimly as he slid slowly along the couch toward her. She was set to run as soon as he got up off the black cushions. Then he was going to have a real job on his hands catching her again.

"Stay away from me, Dev Colter. I haven't made up my mind yet about you!"

"I know. I'm going to help you come to your senses. This game you're playing has gone on long enough, honey. Tonight it ends." He moved a bit closer. The cane, at least, was within reach now. She edged to the side of the hearth, her eyes never leaving him.

"This isn't a game, Dev. Can't you understand? You fooled me once before, and I'm not going to be tricked again."

"I did not trick you!"

"You're not the man I thought you were on that ship!"

"Well, we're even then, because you're not exactly the woman I thought you were, either," he gritted. A couple more inches he told himself. Just a couple more inches.

"What's that supposed to mean?" she blazed, clearly incensed at the accusation.

"It means I'm learning you've got claws, tabby cat. But that's all right, I'll teach you to keep them sheathed around me." Would she break to the right or the left? He eyed her with all his years of experience and decided that this little opponent would dodge to the right. She seemed to put just a shade more weight on that foot when she edged away from the fire. Yes, it would be to the right. He curled his fingers around the handle of the cane and tensed. "Tabby, don't fight me. You know you want this as much as I do."

"I'm still thinking about what you've been saying these past few days, Dev," she informed him aloofly. "And I'm going to take all the time I want deciding what to do."

"You're going to have your mind made up for you tonight," he growled.

"Why?" she demanded aggressively. "Why aren't you willing to give me a little time?"

"Because I have this funny feeling," he returned honestly enough. "A hunch, an *instinct* that something's going to go very wrong if I don't act tonight."

"You're going to rape me because of a hunch?" she exploded.

"You know damn well it's not going to be rape!" The accusation infuriated him. He was going to make love to her, not assault her, and she ought to know that. He wouldn't hurt a hair on her head. Although he might seriously consider taking his belt to her for what she was putting him through tonight, he amended. "Come here, Tabby!"

"It's time you left, Dev."

He feinted, using the cane to lever himself up off the couch. She misinterpreted the direction of his movement and did as Dev had expected, darting to her right. Bracing himself against the curving arm of the black sofa, Dev leaned forward and blocked her path of flight with the ebony cane.

"Damn you!" Tabby swore violently as she ran full tilt into the unexpected barrier of the cane which stretched across her path at the level of her waist. Before she could recover herself Dev swept her back against his chest with the ebony stick. Then he released it as he caught her in his hands.

She pummeled him, throwing herself against his chest in an attempt to force him off balance. Dev didn't try to fight the effort and as a result they both sprawled into a heap in front of the fire. The thick, white sheepskin rug cushioned their fall, although Dev made an effort to absorb most of the impact.

Tabitha landed on top of him, her breath hissing sharply between her teeth. He didn't give her a chance to catch it again. With a swift movement he rolled over, trapping her writhing body beneath his own. He saw the reflection of the firelight in her furious eyes, felt the thrust of her soft curves as she struggled, and his body leaped into vivid awareness.

"Tabby, I want you!" he muttered in husky wonder and then he bent his head to take her mouth. She parted her lips to protest and he took advantage of the opportunity to force himself intimately inside. There was a hint of brandy mingled with the natural warmth of her mouth, and Dev was exhilarated by the heady combination.

He held her easily, his strength and weight pinning her to the sheepskin rug almost effortlessly. With every twisting, struggling movement she only succeeded in arousing him further. His body was pulsating with the sheer pleasure of mastering her softness.

"Damn you, Dev!" she gasped, wrenching her mouth free of his for a moment. "Let me up!"

He lifted his head for an instant to stare down into her flaming eyes. "How can I let you go? I need you too damn much tonight." Then he very deliberately tangled his hand in her hair, holding her head still so that he could explore the line of her throat with his lips.

She raked his leg with her foot, trying to drive the heel of her shoe into his skin. "I'm going to trim your claws, cat," he vowed roughly. Then he used his knee to push her thighs apart. The soft emerald fabric of her dress rode high up on her legs, and Dev felt the warmth of her skin through the silky pantyhose. "The only thing I'm going to let you do with those nice legs is wrap them around me. Stop fighting, tabby cat. You know damn well you belong to me."

"The gentlemanly act sure fades in a hurry when you want something, doesn't it?" she charged between clenched teeth. Tabby got one hand temporarily free and dug her nails into the back of his neck.

"Hell!" he muttered, grabbing at the small, clawing fingers and yanking them to a safe distance. Snagging both of her wrists in one of his fists, he moved his free hand to her breast. "You know you've been asking me to touch you like this. You aren't even

wearing a bra. You wanted me to see just enough of
your softness to drive me out of my mind.''

"No!''

"Yes, Tabby. And I like what I've seen. Now I'm
going to take you. It was only a matter of time before
I had you back in my arms. You knew that.'' Beneath
the green fabric of her dress he could feel the taut
peak of her nipple and he gloried in the response. He
moved his hardening body against hers and groaned
aloud as he felt the waiting softness. So feminine and
inviting. His blood was pounding through his veins
as the anticipation coursed along his nerves.

Eagerly his palm slid down over the curve of her
breast to the contour of her waist and beyond. When
he found the hem of her dress he fastened his mouth
on hers to stifle the protest he knew would be forth-
coming, and then he slipped his fingers boldly up the
inside of her thigh.

"When you wake up in the morning you're not
going to be wearing these,'' he growled, gliding his
fingertips over the nylon of her pantyhose. He found
the apex of her thighs and stroked tantalizingly, teasing her through the slick fabric. "How can you lie
beneath me like this and say you don't want me when
I can feel the heat in you? Tell me you want me,
Tabby. Tell me the truth!''

He wanted to hear the words, Dev realized belatedly. He wanted the reassurance of hearing her call
his name. He wanted her to beg him to take her.
When there was no response he stilled for a moment,
raising his head once more to look down into her face.
She gazed up at him through her lashes, her eyes unreadable and unbelievably mysterious. Her soft mouth

was full and sensually parted as the breath came quickly through her lips. What the hell was she thinking?

For the first time that evening doubt assailed him. Panic suddenly overrode his body's urgent demands. Oh, God, what if she didn't love him? What if she no longer even wanted him? He hadn't counted on this. He had been so sure that her blossoming love could not be turned off at will.

"Tabby! Tabby, say my name," he ordered desperately, his whole body suddenly tense and unmoving. "Say my name," he pleaded harshly. What good would that do? he asked himself in surging panic. But he had to hear her say something, anything. Surely she couldn't have changed completely. God help him if he'd been totally wrong. She *had* to love him.

He knew she was searching his face but he had no knowledge of what she sought in his eyes. The tense stillness gripped them both now. In an agony of suspense Dev waited for some sign that his instincts had not failed him completely where this woman was concerned. He needed her so badly.

"Dev," she whispered, her voice suddenly throaty and deeply inviting. "Love me, Dev. I want you so, darling. Please, Dev…"

With a groan of heady relief and savage ecstasy Dev sank back down, gathering her into his arms. He knew he was talking, saying things he didn't fully comprehend. The words were dark and intimate and exciting. He was promising her everything he could think of, in the manner of impassioned males from the dawn of time. And she twined her arms around his neck and drank the promises from his mouth.

She wanted him; loved him. Everything was all right. Everything was perfect. His fingers shook a little as they found the zipper of the emerald dress and lowered it. Then he was pushing the material up her body and over her head. The fullness of her breasts taunted him as the firelight bathed her skin in gold.

"So lovely," he said in wonder. With a muttered exclamation of need he lowered his mouth to taste the rigid berries which capped her curves. The scent of her skin shot through his senses, sending his head into a spin. Dev could feel her nails on his shoulders and suddenly he was impatient with his own clothing. Heaving himself slightly away, he yanked at the knot of his tie and then, as she watched from beneath slumberous lids, he pulled at the buttons of his shirt.

In another moment he was pushing off the remainder of his clothing, his fully aroused body feeling magnificently free and primitively aggressive. Tabby raised her fingertips to snarl them lovingly in the curling hair on his chest and he sucked in his breath as she let her hand follow the line of hair down below his waist.

"You're driving me wild, honey," he managed shakily. The waistband of her pantyhose gave easily beneath the assault of his fingers. Too easily, he realized ruefully an instant later as the delicate nylon abruptly tore. Almost immediately he forgot the small disaster, losing patience altogether with the tight-fitting fabric. Swiftly he yanked the garment off, leaving it in tatters on the floor. Along with the pantyhose came her scrap of silky panties. At last she was lying naked and open, waiting for him.

"Love me, Tabby," he begged hoarsely as he

stretched out along the length of her in slow delight. "Take me inside of you and warm me with your fire. Let me have all of you tonight. I need you, sweetheart. God, how I need you!"

In answer she wrapped him close, her arms circling his neck and her legs parting to allow him between her thighs. He heard his name on her lips as she kissed his throat and the crooning, inviting sound exploded the last of his restraint.

Gripping her shoulders, he surged against her, about to bury himself in her softness, when suddenly he remembered the way she had hesitated, the first time they made love, before accepting the full force of his masculinity. Above all he did not want to hurt her.

"Tabby?" he rasped.

"Yes, Dev, oh, yes, please!" She sank her nails into his shoulders, urging him to complete the union. Her eyes slitted almost shut.

Dev tried to go slowly, to ease himself into her, but the passion in him was too strong to allow for any further restraint. The need to possess her completely was overwhelming him and he succumbed to it with a fierce, driving energy.

She gasped as he forged deeply into her satiny warmth, but she made no move to resist or draw back. Instead she gripped him more violently than ever and lifted herself to meet the passionate, rhythmic power of his body.

Dev lost himself in the reckless, spinning emotions which enveloped them both. On some level he wanted to master her completely and on another he desired only to give himself up to the loving sensuality she offered. On and on he surged, ricocheting back and forth between the two equally powerful, equally sensual demands, and then he felt her responsive body tighten in that special, magical way.

"That's it, honey," he encouraged savagely, "give yourself to me completely. Let go and come to me. I'll hold you. I'll keep you safe."

"Dev!"

Her body shuddered delicately beneath his, gripping him more tightly than ever and pulling him into the vortex with her. Together they fought the last battle and won and then they were cascading down, down through the night, collapsing onto the sheepskin rug in a damp tangle. Dev kept her tightly against him, knowing he would never, ever let her go. She was his.

It was a long time before she stirred slightly beneath him, her lashes flickering open to reveal the drowsy, remembered sensuality in her eyes. He braced himself on his elbows, a faint smile edging his mouth as he returned the knowing, intimate gaze.

"You're magnificent, Tabby. Utterly magnificent."

"So are you, dragon. Arrogant and demanding but quite magnificent." Her voice was soft and slurred, and Dev's smile widened affectionately.

"Sleepy?"

"Umm. You exhaust me. First you wrestle me to the floor and then you ravish me. It's very exhausting, you know."

"I'm a little tired myself," he confessed dryly.

"Amazing."

"I think it's time we went to bed."

"Yes."

The firelight faded into flickering embers as the two people on the sheepskin rug got slowly to their feet, clinging tightly to each other. Together they walked, arms entwined, down the hall to the bedroom.

"I guess I should sweep you off your feet and carry you to bed," Dev sighed, "but the truth is, if I tried it, I'd probably lose my balance and we'd both wind up on the floor. This damn leg of mine..."

"I didn't notice that leg of yours slowing you down any tonight," Tabby drawled. "I never stood a chance, did I?"

"A chance of escaping me? No," he admitted flatly as they reached the bedroom. "I could never let you go, Tabby." he turned to her as she started to pull down the satin comforter that covered the bed. "Tabby?"

"What is it, Dev?"

"Promise me you'll never let me go, either," he rasped with a renewed sense of urgency.

"I don't seem to have much choice in the matter, do I?" she mused. "Come to bed, Dev."

He hesitated, watching her slide naked between the snowy sheets, and then he followed, reaching out to fold her close. What was wrong with him? he wondered restlessly as he lay in the darkness, absently stroking her shoulder. Why was he still getting those uneasy, prickling sensations? He had Tabby in his arms. He had been so sure that taking her would quiet his anxiety.

But now that his body was no longer clamoring with desire, the old, uneasy feeling was back in full

force. What the hell was wrong? He gripped Tabby
more tightly, seeking comfort. She moved against him
in her sleep, offering that which he needed, and he
sighed and fell asleep beside her.

Ten

For the second time that week Tabitha found herself waking up to the sound of an imperious knock on her front door. At least this time she wasn't waking up with a pounding headache to go with it, she thought wryly, floundering to a sitting position beside the still-sleeping man in her bed.

God, he was magnificent, she thought, drinking in the sight of him as he lay there amid the white sheets. Hard and lean and sleek. If he had a dragon's scales, they would be gleaming in the morning sunlight. As it was, his bronzed skin was dark and tantalizing against the bedclothes. And she loved him. Once he had decided to claim her last night there could have been no other possible outcome to the evening other than the one he had planned. How could she have gone on resisting the man she loved?

The knock came again and with a muttered groan

Tabitha pushed aside the sheets and padded to the closet to find her Chinese silk dressing gown, the one with the dragon embroidered down the back and around the hem. Strange that Dev hadn't awakened. His senses were normally so much more acute than her own. Perhaps he hadn't gone to sleep immediately last night. She had awakened once or twice and found him rather restless beside her. When she had put her arm around him he had drifted back into a deeper slumber. Tabitha had taken a subtle pleasure in offering the small comfort. He seemed to need her as well as desire her.

Surely from such roots love could grow?

Hurrying out into the living room, she wrenched open the front door just as a thin, gray-haired man in a dark three-piece suit raised his hand to knock again. His thin, patrician features were set in remote lines.

For an instant they simply stared at each other without any trace of recognition. Then the older man smiled politely, his hazel eyes cool and aloof.

"Good morning. You must be Tabitha. I'm John Delaney."

"Delaney." Tabitha narrowed her eyes, sweeping the line of his conservative suit and the hard, chillingly polite expression on his face. "From Washington, D.C."

He arched one heavy, gray brow. "I see you know of me."

Tabitha abruptly started to close the door in his face. "Go away, John Delaney. You're in the wrong place. This is Washington, state of. Go back to D.C."

He shoved one polished, black shoe over the

threshold, blocking the door. "I gather you know why I'm here."

She lifted her chin with fierce determination, her hand clenching into a small fist. "He's not going back with you, Mr. Delaney. He belongs here now. He belongs to me."

"Come now, Tabitha," Delaney murmured. "If you know Dev Colter at all well, you know he doesn't belong to anyone."

"He does now!" She pushed at the door again but the black shoe didn't move.

"What the hell?" Dev's question cracked across the room and Tabitha whirled to see him standing in the hall doorway. He was wearing only his slacks, which he must have just grabbed off the floor. He was still fastening the belt and yanking up the zipper. "Delaney," he muttered, coming forward far enough to see who stood on the threshold. "I should have known. No wonder I couldn't get that damn uneasy feeling out of my system last night. My instincts were right. As usual."

Delaney smiled, a speculative gleam in his hazel eyes. "Your instincts have always bordered on the precognitive. That's one of the things which makes you so valuable."

Tabitha gasped. "You're clairvoyant?" she demanded in astonishment, staring at Dev as if she hadn't quite seen him clearly before.

He frowned in annoyance. "No, of course not. I just get these hunches occasionally. Usually when something is about to go wrong. I had a feeling something was about to go wrong last night, but I thought..." He broke off. "Well, why are you here, Delaney? Just happen to be on the West Coast?"

"Why, yes, as a matter of fact," John Delaney began soothingly, inching his way through the door.

"Don't believe him," Tabitha ordered Dev. "He's here to get you back to Washington, D.C." She glared at Delaney, who took no notice.

"The little jaunt to the Caribbean should have reassured you that you've still got what it takes, Dev," Delaney murmured smoothly, focusing all his attention on the other man. "You not only got the film for us, you took care of Waverly, too. We knew there was a new independent working the Caribbean region, but we had been unable to smoke him out. Handing him over to us was a nice bonus from you, Dev. We appreciate it."

"Your gratitude overwhelms me."

Tabitha switched her glare from Delaney to Dev. What was the matter with him? Why wasn't he telling the other man to get lost? Dev had made his decision.

Hadn't he?

All of a sudden fear lurched within her stomach. Had Dev only been playing with her? Had he been using her as a pleasant interlude before returning to a job with John Delaney? *Why wasn't he kicking Delaney out of the house?*

"Come now, Dev, you know it's time you stopped fooling around with that travel agency bit and with attractive, young women like Miss Graham. It's time you came back to work, back to what you do best."

Dev looked at him, his face totally unreadable. Tabitha waited in an agony of suspense. Was he really considering going back to Delaney's horrible department?

"No!" she burst out furiously. Dev swung his unreadable gaze to her tense face. "You're not going with him, Dev."

"I'm not?"

"You're a *travel* agent now, not a...a *secret* agent, remember?"

"Actually," Delaney interrupted easily, "his travel agency work makes an excellent cover..."

"It's not a cover!" Tabitha stormed, advancing on the older man with her hands curled violently at her sides. "It's his job! His career! Furthermore, he's going to be a married man, soon. He can't be running around doing your dirty work for you. Not anymore!"

Delaney eyed her as if she was finally beginning to pose a mild threat. "Married?"

"That's right. I'm marrying him, Mr. Delaney, and I will not allow him to go on risking his life in dark alleys and mazes..."

"Mazes?" Delaney looked a little blank.

"Or anywhere else, for that matter! He's going to open a nice little shop next to my bookstore and he's going to sell airline tickets and cruise ship tours and that's all! He will be home every night, sitting right here in front of my hearth wearing slippers and sipping sherry. He's most definitely not going to be running your stupid errands or risking his neck. Do I make myself very clear, Mr. Delaney?"

Delaney stared at her now as if she were some strange, new animal. Then he glanced at Dev. "Where the hell did you find her?"

"I didn't find her. She found me. She rescued me from an alley on St. Regis."

"I found him and I'm going to keep him!" Tabitha blazed.

"Are you?" Delaney flicked another speculative glance at her, and then he pinned Dev with a cool, probing glance. "She seems quite determined to rescue you again. This time from me." There was a significant pause and then the older man asked almost gently, "Do you really want to be rescued from me, Dev?"

Tabitha, stricken, stared at Dev, too. There was not much she could do if Dev Colter didn't want to be rescued this time. Her heart raced anxiously as she held her breath. Her whole future hung in the balance. What would she do if Dev walked out with his old boss this morning? The heart which was pounding so nervously would break this time. She could not bear to lose him now.

"Dev," she whispered starkly. "I love you."

He looked at her. "Do you, Tabby?"

"With all my heart."

The sudden flare of warmth in his silver eyes seemed to light the whole room. "I won't be going anywhere, tabby cat. I think I've been in love with you since you dragged me out of that damn St. Regis alley. All I want is a home here with you."

"Oh, Dev!" Tabitha managed to unstick her feet from the floor and hurl herself into Dev's arms. He caught her, staggering a bit under the impact, but his braced feet supported them both while she buried her face against his chest and wrapped her arms around his bare waist.

Over the top of her head Dev smiled crookedly at his former boss. "You need a new, young dragon, Delaney. I'm afraid I've lost my taste for your kind of work. I wasn't altogether sure of that when I agreed to take the Caribbean job for you, but now I'm quite positive."

"I see," Delaney said with unexpected softness in his voice. "You do seem to have made up your mind. Strange, I never saw you as the home-and-hearth type."

"Home and hearth complete with my own tabby cat," Dev said, chuckling, his hand lightly stroking Tabitha's hair as she continued to cling to him. "You ought to try it sometime, Delaney. You don't know what you've missed."

Delaney watched the way Tabitha was holding his former agent. "How much of your past is she aware of?"

Tabitha turned her head to glare at Delaney. "It's not his past I'm concerned with, it's his present and his future."

"Dev?" Delaney made one last appeal.

"My present and my future are here in Washington, state of, Delaney," Dev said with quiet conviction.

"You're sure, aren't you?"

"Very."

Delaney sighed. "I was afraid of that. But it was worth a try. I don't suppose," he went on matter-of-factly, "that anyone would like to fix me a cup of coffee before you throw me out of the house?"

Tabitha slowly freed herself from Dev's grasp, eyeing her foe with deep suspicion. But John Delaney merely smiled pleasantly.

"It's okay, Tabitha. I know when I've lost. He's all yours. Wouldn't do me much good, anyway, if he kept thinking of you every time I sent him into the field. Being in love blunts a man's instincts."

"Not all of them," Dev retorted dryly, but he was suddenly grinning. "Come on, Delaney, I'll fix you a cup of coffee."

"Thank you. I need something warm. It certainly rains a lot here in Washington, state of, doesn't it?"

"Yeah," Dev agreed easily, "but somehow it never seems as cold here as it does in Washington, D.C."

That evening Tabitha curled happily against Dev as they sat on one of the black sofas in front of the fire. She hadn't really relaxed until John Delaney was on a plane heading back to Washington, D.C., but now her world seemed warm and right. Dreamily she ran her fingers through Dev's dark hair. His arm tightened around her in response.

"Thank you for rescuing me again, tabby cat," he drawled, nuzzling her earlobe with lazy anticipation. "That's twice now. I'm going to be in your debt for the rest of my life."

"Exactly where I want you," she teased, her eyes alive with love.

"I love you," he murmured simply.

"When did you first realize it?" she demanded.

"When I walked out of the bedroom this morning and found you trying to kick Delaney out of the house. I suppose I'd been in love all along, but the sight of you tangling with John Delaney for my sake made me put a name to it. Up until then I'd been thinking in terms of wanting and needing. But it all came together for me this morning. What about you, honey?''

"I knew I loved you that night I seduced you on the boat," she admitted with a ready smile.

"I kept telling myself you must love me, but when you skipped the island after that scene with Waverly I was afraid I was going to have a hell of a time getting you to admit you felt something for me. Then when I arrived here and found that young cub asleep on your living room couch and discovered you were bent on trying to forget me, I wanted to tear Port Townsend apart. Tabby, I may not have understood right away that what I felt for you was love, but I did know right away that I needed you desperately. Your love was what had been missing from my life. I could never let you go, sweetheart.''

"I'll never want to leave you, dragon. You are my very own, very fabulous beast." She raised her face invitingly, winding her arms around his neck.

"Are you about to seduce me again?" he demanded, silver eyes turning smoky with stirring desire.

"I'm engaged in a bit of research."

"Research on what?"

"On the mating habits of dragons."

"I can tell you one thing for sure about this particular dragon," Dev vowed as he lowered his mouth to hers. "This beast has just mated for life."

* * * * *

#1 *New York Times* bestselling author

NORA ROBERTS

introduces the loyal and loving, tempestuous and tantalizing Stanislaski family.

Coming in November 2000:

The Stanislaski Brothers
Mikhail and Alex

Their immigrant roots and warm, supportive home had made Mikhail and Alex Stanislaski both strong and passionate. And their charm makes them irresistible....

In February 2001, watch for
THE STANISLASKI SISTERS: *Natasha and Rachel*

And a brand-new Stanislaski story from Silhouette Special Edition,
CONSIDERING KATE

Available at your favorite retail outlet.

Where love comes alive™

Visit Silhouette at www.eHarlequin.com   PSSTANBR2

You're not going to believe this offer!

**In October and November 2000, buy any two Harlequin
or Silhouette books and save $10.00 off future purchases,
or buy any three and save $20.00 off future purchases!**

Just fill out this form and attach 2 proofs of purchase (cash register
receipts) from October and November 2000 books and Harlequin will
send you a coupon booklet worth a total savings of $10.00 off future
purchases of Harlequin and Silhouette books in 2001. Send us 3 proofs
of purchase and we will send you a coupon booklet worth a total
savings of $20.00 off future purchases.

Saving money has never been this easy.

I accept your offer! Please send me a coupon booklet:

Name: _____

Address: _____ City: _____

State/Prov.: _____ Zip/Postal Code: _____

Optional Survey!

In a typical month, how many Harlequin or Silhouette books would you buy <u>new</u> at retail stores?

☐ Less than 1 ☐ 1 ☐ 2 ☐ 3 to 4 ☐ 5+

Which of the following statements best describes how you <u>buy</u> Harlequin or Silhouette books?
Choose one answer only that <u>best</u> describes you.

☐ I am a regular buyer and reader
☐ I am a regular reader but buy only occasionally
☐ I only buy and read for specific times of the year, e.g. vacations
☐ I subscribe through Reader Service but also buy at retail stores
☐ I mainly borrow and buy only occasionally
☐ I am an occasional buyer and reader

Which of the following statements best describes how you <u>choose</u> the Harlequin and Silhouette
series books you buy <u>new</u> at retail stores? By "series," we mean books within a particular line,
such as *Harlequin PRESENTS* or *Silhouette SPECIAL EDITION*. Choose one answer only that
<u>best</u> describes you.

☐ I only buy books from my favorite series
☐ I generally buy books from my favorite series but also buy
books from other series on occasion
☐ I buy some books from my favorite series but also buy from
many other series regularly
☐ I buy all types of books depending on my mood and what
I find interesting and have no favorite series

Please send this form, along with your cash register receipts as proofs of purchase, to:
In the U.S.: Harlequin Books, P.O. Box 9057, Buffalo, NY 14269
In Canada: Harlequin Books, P.O. Box 622, Fort Erie, Ontario L2A 5X3
(Allow 4-6 weeks for delivery) Offer expires December 31, 2000.

PHQ4002